Tag. You're it.

Odie felt him look her o... head moved down a little, which is... him away. She was in a white cotton T-shirt and white-washed jeans. Nothing sexy about it, but she still felt like a silly girl, infatuated and eager to flirt.

"Get what you needed?" he asked with a hint of amusement.

"How did you know I was here?" she asked.

"Lucky guess." He pushed off the car, straightening his tall form. "You know, you're going to have to start trusting me."

Odie reached into her tote and pulled out the GPS device and handed it to him. He opened his palm for her to drop it there.

She tipped her head back, putting her face close to his. "I do trust you."

A grin spread over his mouth, showing off straight, white teeth. He really had to stop with the sex-appeal thing.

★ ★ ★

Dear Reader,

At long last, here it is—Odelia Frank's story! Of all the secondary characters who've colored the pages of All McQueen's Men books, I can't think of any other who deserves it more than her.

When I first created Odie's character in *The Secret Soldier,* I did it to push Cullen McQueen. Drive his story and bring it to resolution. I needed a strong woman who functioned both as his smart, savvy and quite capable intel officer and his friend.

Throughout the miniseries, Odie has done a fine job helping Tactical Executive Security operatives accomplish their missions, supplying them necessary intelligence with her sassy tongue and tempting them with her beauty. Tough, smart and, yes, bold and brash Odelia Frank doesn't have anyone to tease about love in this story. She's got trouble of her own right now—and a man to go with it!

So, sit back and enjoy the story of TES's number-one intel officer, and find out what changes are made to the best counterterror organization in the world by the end.

Jennie

JENNIFER MOREY

Special Ops Affair

ROMANTIC

SUSPENSE

Recycling programs
for this product may
not exist in your area.

ISBN-13: 978-0-373-27723-0

SPECIAL OPS AFFAIR

Printed in U.S.A.

Books by Jennifer Morey

Romantic Suspense

★*The Secret Soldier* #1526
★*Heiress Under Fire* #1578
Blackout at Christmas #1583
"Kiss Me on Christmas"
★*Unmasking the Mercenary* #1606
The Librarian's Secret Scandal #1624
★*Special Ops Affair* #1653

★All McQueen's Men

JENNIFER MOREY

Two-time 2009 RITA® Award nominee and a Golden Quill winner for Best First Book for *The Secret Soldier,* Jennifer Morey writes contemporary romance and romantic suspense. Project manager du jour, she works for the space systems segment of a satellite imagery and information company and lives in sunny Denver, Colorado. She can be reached through her website, www.jennifermorey.com, and on Facebook—jmorey2009@gmail.com.

To my readers. With Odie's story, it's only appropriate that this is the only dedication I need. Thank you for your support. Thank you for loving my stories. And thank you for asking me to write new ones about characters featured in my miniseries.

Chapter 1

It wasn't that she didn't like nerds. It wasn't. Odelia Frank eyed Cullen McQueen and the new guy, Jagger Benney, mixed with angst and resignation. She was tired of Cullen's teasing and Jag's quiet absorption of it all. She couldn't even complain. Normally it was her doing the teasing, but now it was coming back around.

"I didn't love him," she argued, realizing she'd folded her arms. It was so uncharacteristically defensive of her. She lowered them to her sides. What did she care what these two thought?

"Didn't you know that *before* you were standing on the altar next to him?" Cullen asked, his grin annoying the crap out of her.

No. She'd thought she loved him up until then.

Jag hadn't said anything since Cullen started in on her. He never said much, only when he had to. He never responded to her well-placed barbs, either, and she suspected that was because he didn't like it or hadn't quite figured her out yet. Didn't matter. He was the epitome of what had driven her to nearly marry a nerd.

Standing about an inch shorter than Cullen's towering six-five, he had the same he-man build. His arms bulged and that white T-shirt stretched over his impressive chest. And was he trying to be stylish with those holes in the thigh and knee of his faded jeans? Please. It was almost funny. Big, bad special ops dude, looking good enough for a Calvin Klein ad.

He watched her with glowing green eyes, as if he was always sizing her up. That's why she was leaning toward *hadn't figured her out yet*. If she wasn't so immune to guys like him she'd be uncomfortable. He studied her like a textbook.

"What…no comment?" Cullen said. "Don't tell me I've actually cracked that shell of yours."

Odie swung her attention back to him. "You're enjoying this."

"Oh, yeah." His smile spread wider across his face.

"All right, so I took pity on him."

"Took pity?" He chuckled. "I doubt he'll ever recover. You blew into his life like a hurricane and then blew right back out."

"It wasn't that bad." Was it? Had she hurt her sweet nerdy boyfriend that much?

"No, not that bad. At least you took him off the altar to break his heart."

She'd taken him to an antechamber in the church and told him she couldn't marry him. She thought he'd handled it pretty well. He'd be upset for a little while, but he'd get over it. "I did the right thing."

Cullen didn't even have to say anything. The way he

shook his head said it all. She should have broken if off before the wedding. The Odie he knew didn't make mistakes like that.

But what he wasn't giving her credit for was that her fiancé thought she was good for him, when she wasn't. He was lucky she'd come to her senses. Once the honeymoon was over he'd have seen the unabridged, tenacious, controlling side of her. She'd have made him miserable. It didn't pain her to admit that.

"He would have spent the rest of his life doing what I told him." She tried to make him understand. "What man wants that from a woman? I did him a favor."

"Don't get me wrong—I agree."

Odie took no insult. That was the way she and Cullen communicated. He knew her better than anyone.

Jag walked over to the window and looked outside, presenting the back of his head and thick, light brown hair. He appeared bored, but she knew he wasn't. She'd like to know what was going on in his head. The fact that she was curious disconcerted her a little.

She followed his feigned interest through the window. It was a spectacular late September day in the Rockies. A comfortable sixty-five degrees at more than nine-thousand feet. Colorado was a great place to live that way. There were days in the middle of winter when the temperature warmed enough to go without a jacket, even up here. As soon as the sun set, however, all bets were off. She found that she liked the unpredictable weather here. But she could do without the isolation of small mountain town living. Maybe she'd never forgive Cullen for locating his headquarters here. She preferred the pollution and busy rudeness of Washington, D.C.

Jag turned to look at her then, catching her watching

him. Their gazes caught and he grew more alert, aware of her. Was that curiosity she saw? It was the first time she'd ever seen any kind of reaction in those watchful green eyes of his. Usually they revealed nothing but the shrewd workings of a daring mind.

He'd been here a month and already he'd gone on one mission. It hadn't taken him long. Just a few days to find and take out their target. She wondered what his story was. What had driven him to become an American hero? Cullen had found him through a friend at the CIA. Jag was a Navy SEAL who'd moved on to work with the CIA. Good with languages. Familiar with the Middle East. He had all the prerequisites Cullen demanded from his team. And everything Odie refused to involve herself with romantically. No man like that could give her what she needed. Least of all marriage. Although lately Cullen's operatives had been marrying left and right. First Cullen— and boy had that been a shocker—then Elam Rhule, and most recently Haley Engen. The love they had for their partners appeared to be strong enough to last, too.

Maybe it was just she who couldn't marry a TES operative. None of them could handle her sarcasm, for one thing, and daredevil egos drove her insane for another. She should know. She'd tried it once. She'd married an operative and a few months later he was killed in action. It had affected her more deeply than she'd ever imagined. How much she'd loved him. If it hadn't been for his damn career, they'd still be married because he'd still be alive. That's what always got to her, the thoughts of what might have been. There would never be another Sage for her.

Realizing she'd been staring at Jag this whole time and that he hadn't missed a second of it, she turned away.

"I'll be honored to meet the man who can handle you,"

Cullen said, his face sober now. He knew her history and had probably guessed where her thoughts had wandered.

"When are you going to tell me why you dragged me in here on my day off?" she snapped. Enough of all this focus on her personal affairs. They had work to do.

Cullen grunted a short laugh and shook his head. "You're an amazing woman, Odie. You know that?"

She rolled her eyes, though his compliments always made her feel good.

"I need you to brief Jag on the Defense Initiatives assignment," he said.

That got her brow lifting. She slid her gaze to Jag and his appearance of cool observation. "Are you going to work that one for Cullen?"

"Yes."

There he went again, full of words. Some day she was going to have to make him say more. While she wondered why she even had the urge, she asked, "What has Cullen told you so far?"

"He said you'd fill me in."

Vague reply for something she was sure he knew more about than he was letting on. Sage had been like that. Smart.

Getting aggravated with her wandering interest, Odie opened her file cabinet and pulled out the correct file. She had everything on her computer, but paper copies were always handy at times like this. She gave Jag the file.

"Hersch is founder and CEO of Defense Initiatives," she began to narrate. "He's got an office in Washington, D.C., apparently to stay close to his political clientele, but he has houses in other places. A real winner of a guy. Records himself having sex with more than one woman at a time. Has an entire library of videos locked away in his house, in fact. Been arrested for drugs. Two DUIs. Married and divorced three times. He's forty-nine but in pretty good physical shape if you can ignore his growing stomach. Not the most attractive fellow. Probably had to pay all those women to sleep with him and I bet none of them knew they were porn stars for a day."

"How did he get into arms brokering?" Jag asked.

"Ex-military. Army lieutenant. Before he was slapped on the hand and discharged for sexual misconduct, anyway."

"What is of concern, here," Cullen interrupted, "is that a lot of his contracts come from the U.S. government to legitimately sell arms to places like Afghanistan."

"Right," Odie said. "But we got a tip that he's been doing business with an Albanian military export company that frequently obtains their inventory from China to save money. The buyer doesn't always know."

"As you can imagine, we can't have that hitting the press," Cullen said.

Jag looked at Odie while he appeared to absorb it all. "How did you find out he had the recordings?"

Of all the questions she'd expected, that wasn't one of them. "I have more friends than he does."

"In other words, don't ask," Cullen said.

Jag glanced from him to her.

"She's got contacts in places you'll never guess, so don't even try. She won't give their names or identities away, either, for obvious reasons. They trust her. Nobody who talks to her is going to die because of it."

"So I've heard," Jag said, sounding strangely complimentary. But was it professional respect or personal interest she heard?

Who had he been talking to? She looked at Cullen. She

wouldn't put it past him. But what bothered her was that she liked it. Jag had asked about her. He must have. And she liked that? Her armor rose up.

"I don't mix business with pleasure," she said. Just in case.

A half grin lifted his mouth. "I've heard that, too."

She was too stunned by the transformation on his face to respond. Intending to ignore him, she picked up her work tote and slung the strap over her shoulder. Before heading to the door, she stopped in front of Cullen.

"What are you planning to do with Hersch?"

"Send Jag for a job interview. Once he's inside he can confirm or put to rest our suspicions. Based on what he finds, we'll take action from there."

A recon mission. She glanced at Jag. Was that going to be enough of a rush for him? It didn't seem very dangerous for a man like him. This assignment was small-scale compared to most TES missions.

"And I want you to work with him. I want you available 24/7. This isn't like our other assignments. We're on U.S. soil and Jag is going to need access to information whenever he needs it. Morning. Noon. Night."

"I'm available 24/7 now, so why would Jag's job be any different?" At least she'd only have to communicate with him over the phone and in email.

"I want it to be your only focus."

The small scale of the mission didn't match the urgency. But she knew Cullen and how he operated. So she didn't question him.

"Is that it for today?"

"Yes."

"See you later, then." Without acknowledging Jag, she reached the door.

"Oh, and Odie?"

She paused and turned back.

"See if you can find someone close to Hersch. Someone who'd talk if we gave them a little push."

"Already on my to-do list." She tapped the side of her head with a smile.

She left the building, trying to dismiss the effect Jag had on her. Somehow he seemed different than other TES operatives. Usually they tried to hit on her, backing off only when they discovered her tongue was too sharp for kissing. Jag had not only never hit on her, he seemed to see right through her. Did he already know it was futile? The very idea of that tantalized her. She thought about it all the way home. It was only a two-minute drive in this puny mountain town.

Pulling into her driveway, Odie parked in the garage and went to get the mail. There was a lot. Mostly junk, but a couple of bills and a thick manila envelope. Closing the garage door, she entered the house. In the kitchen, she dumped her tote and mail on the snack bar and went to the refrigerator for a beer.

After sipping the Warsteiner, she set the bottle on the snack bar and went to her bedroom to change her clothes. Once inside she stopped and turned back to the open door. She usually shut it in the mornings. She liked her bedroom cool at night, so she closed the registers. She searched the room. Nothing seemed out of place.

Something flapping on the other side of the window caught her eye. She moved closer. The screen was torn. She touched the lock on the window. It was secure.

She stared at the bedroom door. Maybe she'd just forgotten. Even though she never did....

She didn't own a gun anymore and had stopped practicing

firing one. Everyone at TES would be surprised to know that. When her husband was killed, guns had become a symbol of loss. But now she wished she'd been able to let go of that old tenet.

Shaking that thought away along with all it threatened to dredge up, she decided to stay in her short-sleeved purple blouse, faded jeans and hiking boots. She walked out of the bedroom, feeling like an idiot for being scared. This was Roaring Creek, for God's sake. The only crime that happened here was jaywalking. Well, ever since Cullen had arrived, that is. No one dared to misbehave with him around.

She peeked into her office. Nothing out of place. No one lurking in the bathroom, either. She entered her living room. No sounds. No shadows. No sign of movement.

She breathed a sigh of relief. Shaking her head, she went to the snack bar and took a sip of her beer. The package in the pile of mail caught her attention. It was addressed to her, of course, but it was the return address that made her go still for a second. It was a P.O. Box from Washington, D.C. One she knew very well. The initials above it gave her hand a tremor as she put the beer down. Brow tightening, she lifted the package and tore open the top.

Creaking floorboards sent her heart skittering. She dropped the package and spun to face the living room. The sound had come from behind her in the hallway. She looked toward the dining area. It had two entrances, one from the living room and the other from the kitchen. A wall partially blocked her view of the dining area. She moved to peer around the wall. Nothing.

She shut her eyes and breathed deep a few times. What had her so spooked? Nobody was after her. Her identity was protected through TES. She gathered information from trusted sources, sources that were anonymous and would never expose her. She made sure of that. There was no reason for anyone to come after her. Unless there was a burglar. But not only was her house locked, she didn't have anything worth stealing. A couple of slinky cocktail dresses and a wedding ring she no longer wore. She didn't even have a nice TV. Computer. Okay, that was nice, but she'd seen it in her office, right as she'd left it this morning.

No one was in her house and no one had stolen anything. Maybe she was just tired.

Going back to the snack bar, she saw the manila envelope and had second thoughts. She glanced once more around the living room, unable to shake the feeling that she wasn't alone. Or, even more disturbing, the significance of the initials on the package. If the package was what she thought it was, someone could have a damn good reason to come after her.

Steadying her quickening breaths, she parted the opening in the package and slid out a clipped stack of papers. The top one was a picture of Hersch. She recognized him instantly. The hairs on the back of her neck prickled her with eerie foreboding. The file had come from one of her most trusted sources. The initials...

Something was wrong.

What did Hersch have to do with ELF? The magnitude of it wrapped around her mind and bombarded her with unanswered questions.

Glancing behind her, she lifted the first page to reveal another photo. This man she didn't recognize. He stood outside a coffee shop, near the front door and next to a railing that bordered an outdoor patio. He was looking up the street. It was a full facial shot. He was an older man, probably in his fifties, maybe closer to sixty.

A sound from her left sent her pulse ricocheting in her chest. She faced the dining area. Someone was in there. She felt it. Sensed a presence. Dropping the papers and manila envelope onto the countertop, she started backing away.

A man dressed in black and wearing a ski mask appeared in the entrance to her kitchen.

He was big, with a barrel stomach and hulking shoulders. He'd come from the dining room. How had she missed him? Where had he been hiding?

He advanced toward her, moving around the snack bar. She pivoted and ran for the door. He was faster, leaping in front of her and blocking her escape, standing between her and the door. Panting for air, she backed into the living room, searching for some kind of a weapon. Could she make it to the kitchen drawer where she kept her knives? The lamp in her living room was too heavy to use as a club. She looked at the masked man again. He pulled a gun from a holster on his thigh.

Blood left her face, giving her skin a stark chill. Her pulse jackhammered. He didn't say anything, which was creepier than if he had. Asking him what he wanted was moot. Obviously he was here because he knew about the package. It didn't take much of a stretch to figure out he didn't want her or anyone else to know about the contents.

She kept backing up and he kept advancing. When she reached the threshold of the dining area, she turned and ran around the wall into the kitchen. She made it to the knife drawer. The man strode toward her through the kitchen. She had to abandon grabbing a knife when she saw him swing his gun to hit her on the head. She moved, but he caught her with a hard blow.

She staggered. He raised his gun for another blow. She

blocked the strike with her forearm. Pain shot all the way up to her shoulder.

Stomping as hard as she could on his instep, she rammed her elbow into his solar plexus. He grunted and stumbled backward. She turned and swung her leg to kick him in the head, but he was quicker and blocked her with his arm and then swiped her off balance. Her head hit the edge of the snack bar as she fell to the floor.

Dizzy, she crawled backward, trying to get around the snack bar, closer to the door. The masked man stepped toward her, leaning as he swung his gun again. She blocked the strike with her arm, more pain stinging her. He lost his grip on the gun. It skidded over the snack bar and landed on the living room floor.

With a growl, he formed a fist and tried to punch her. She blocked him again. What was he trying to do? Knock her out? Yeah, and then take her somewhere remote to kill her. What was in that package? It must be something big.

She crawled backward again, making it into the living room. He easily followed, coming alongside her and kicking her in the ribs. She shouted in pain. He hit her, his knuckles smashing the side of her head. Dots of light sprinkled her vision.

Real fear overwhelmed her. He was a professional. It was too easy for him to overpower her and his moves were sure and practiced. She didn't have time to grapple with the implications. The photo…a professional hit man after her…those initials…

He struck her again. She rolled onto her stomach and pushed herself up, trying to get leverage before he succeeded in knocking her out. Fear was a foreign emotion to her, but now she felt its tentacles trying to reach past her strength and choke her. He struck her head once more.

Slumping to the floor, unable to support her own weight, she despaired. She was going to black out.

Her attacker must have thought she already had. With her cheek to the carpeted floor, she watched him snatch the still-clipped papers from the counter and stuff them inside his tucked-in, black button-up shirt. He then picked up his gun from the floor and straightened, turning to face her. Odie pretended to be unconscious. He approached. When he reached her, he grabbed her ankles and dragged her through the living room.

He was going to kidnap her. She couldn't let him, but she was too weak right now. She needed her head to clear a little more. She'd wait for an opportunity. Then she'd escape. If the worst happened and she couldn't, then no matter how brutally he tortured her, she could not tell him a thing.

Jag parked down the street, scanning his surroundings as he got out of his Volkswagen Jetta. If he had to work with Odie, they were going to get a few things straight. He wasn't going to put up with her smart mouth anymore. She was going to have to respect him, at least for the duration of the mission. Then she could go back to her sweet, hissing self.

She lived in the northeastern section of Roaring Creek, close to downtown—what there was of it. Most houses here were older. Newer ones were located outside of town.

Taking in the deep green paint and tasteful beige-tan trim and the immaculate yard, he was momentarily surprised. He'd have never guessed a woman like her would be interested in gardening, but he could tell by the neatly trimmed plants that in summer the front yard would explode with color. Her covered front porch had quaint wicker furniture, too.

Nothing Cullen had told him about her, or that he'd observed, could have prepared him for this glimpse of a softer side. So much piss and vinegar laced her sharp intelligence that it was hard for him to imagine any depth to her femininity. The first time he'd seen her he'd thought of girly magazines and burlesque shows. Two seconds later he'd been put in his place.

Good thing his thoughts had been just that. Thoughts. He'd stopped his purely male interest from showing in time. The contrast between her body and her brain was a thing of marvel. He'd gotten tangled with women like her before. They weren't as intimidating as Odie could be, but they were in the same line of work. He'd also gotten tangled with the sheltered civilian type. And he couldn't forget the closet rebel he'd married without knowing she was a closet rebel until it was too late. That had been the last attempt he'd made at having a relationship with a woman. He'd wait until he was sure next time.

Something about Odie's tough exterior bothered him, anyway. It was almost as if she were hiding the real her. And after his last relationship, that never settled well with him. He preferred women who were more of an open book. Easier to spot a lie that way.

He stepped up the three stairs, his tactical boots thudding on the wood planks. A thumping sound from the garage followed by a human grunt propelled him into combat mode. The noise sounded like it came from a man. It definitely wasn't Odie.

Instinct kicked into gear. He never ignored his instinct. He bent and pulled out the pistol he kept tucked in his boot when he wasn't working. Testing the door handle, he found it unlocked. He pushed the door open, swinging his aim as he entered. A snack bar separated the kitchen from the living room. Dining room straight ahead. The door leading to the garage was open. He could hear the outer, larger one finish opening.

He hurried there, pausing at the doorway to peer into the garage. Odie's truck was backing out of the garage. She wasn't driving. He couldn't see her. Where was she? He moved down the two steps into the garage with his pistol raised, aiming at the driver. A masked man. The driver saw him and ducked just as Jag fired, and then raced the vehicle out of the driveway.

Jag didn't fire again. He didn't want to risk hitting Odie. Was she in the cab? Had the masked man killed her? Should he check the house or go after the truck? He wouldn't have time to check the house if he went after the truck. Movement in the bed of the truck had him running for his car. Strands of dark hair. Odie.

Slamming his car door shut, he saw the truck disappear around a corner down the street. He revved the Jetta engine and charged after it.

Turning the corner, he saw the truck turn again, heading for the highway. He pushed his Jetta as fast as it would go.

Odie's head appeared over the edge of the truck's tailgate. She looked behind her, into the cab of the truck and then at him. Her long hair whipped about her head. The driver looked in his rearview mirror. He drove faster along the curving mountainous road, an attempt to keep Odie from jumping out of the truck.

Odie hung on to the tailgate, letting go briefly to point to the ground, jabbing her finger two or three times.

He shook his head. "Don't even think about it."

She jabbed her finger three more times, nodding adamantly. Damn it. She was going to jump. Jag gripped the steering wheel tighter, not taking his gaze off her.

The truck slowed into a turn. Odie swung a leg over the top of the tailgate.

"Don't jump out now." Damn woman. Was she crazy?

The truck's brake lights lit. Jag slammed on his own brakes as the truck fishtailed with Odie clinging to the tailgate. The masked man slowed the truck more and Jag saw the forest access road ahead. He followed the truck as it turned there.

The masked man raised a gun and awkwardly aimed behind him, shooting out the rear window, missing Odie but putting a hole in Jag's windshield on the passenger's side.

Odie jumped off the truck, rolling over the top of the tailgate and tumbling to the ground.

Jag cursed and swerved to avoid running her over and then skidded the car to a halt. He was about to get out to help her when the passenger door opened and she climbed inside, grunting in what had to be pain.

"Go, go, go!" she yelled.

But he'd already floored the gas pedal, following the dust trail the truck had left behind. Glancing over at her, he saw a bruise emerging on her alabaster cheek. "Are you okay?"

"Why? You want to hold me while I cry about it?"

There she went again, hissing. All part of her armor. One he was beginning to want to crack.

"Don't worry. I know better," he said drily.

"We have to catch that truck."

"I'm working on it." The dust trail was plenty for him to follow.

"Don't lose him." She sounded urgent. More urgent than necessary. He didn't need to be told to go after the truck. What did she think he was doing? Going for a joyride?

There had always been something different about her. And not just her brassy way of bulldozing her way through life. There was something else. Something about her that he couldn't quite pinpoint. And he had a sneaking suspicion whoever was driving that truck would open a big clue.

The dust trail grew thicker and Jag knew he was gaining. The road narrowed. He had to slow down. The road wound its way to some abandoned mines, but as it climbed in elevation, the cliffs grew more precarious along its crumbling edge. Odie's attacker wouldn't get far anyway. The road would dead end and he'd be trapped.

The road curved and Jag spotted the truck ahead. It was moving fast, too fast for the width of the road. He felt it coming before it happened. The truck skidded, fishtailed, its rear tire catching the edge of the road. It pulled the vehicle over the cliff.

Odie's sharp inhale resonated in the car, followed by a soft, "No."

He wondered about the degree of her urgency as the truck hit the side of the mountain and violently flipped through the air as it hurled to the rocky canyon floor. Jag stopped his car as a plume of fire erupted upon impact.

Odie scrambled out of the car and rushed to the edge of the road, watching with her mouth open and dark eyes wide. He got out to stand beside her.

"We have to get down there," she said, starting to walk along the road, searching for a place to climb down.

He took hold of her arm and stopped her. "We can't." It was too steep.

"You don't understand." She shrugged free of his hold. "He took something. Someone sent me a package that contained information about Hersch. That's why he came here."

That might explain her urgency. "What information?"

She didn't seem to hear him. She kept looking for a place to climb down the steep mountainside.

"What information, Odie?"

She glanced at him. "About Hersch."

Her hesitation and evasive reply raised his suspicion.

"You said that. What kind of information about him?"

He watched her stare down at the licking flames as if willing them to go out. He'd buy that she was a little stunned after her near-death experience, but she was acting strange. He didn't think her ordeal was the only thing that had her shaken.

Jag looked into the yawning canyon. "Pretty big fire."

"He had the back of the truck rigged to blow." Her concentration barely deviated, her response sounding automatic.

"Better to roast you with once he got what he wanted."

Her gaze found his for a brief moment, long enough for him to see she'd already considered that but was having a hard time accepting it.

"Why was he after you?"

"I don't know."

He didn't believe her. "Who was he?"

Her eyes lost their tinge of desperate determination and the Odie he was more familiar with resurfaced. "Don't be a smart-ass."

"Who was he?" he repeated. She knew damn well he'd stopped being smart and was now asking her legitimate questions.

"How the hell should I know?"

Jag had always been careful about what he said in front of their stoic and fair-to-a-fault boss, but the more he watched Odie, the more he thought there were things about her no one knew. Now he got the impression she was holding something important back and it confirmed his hunch.

"You didn't recognize him?" he asked.

"He was wearing a mask."

She wasn't lying about that. She didn't know who'd attacked her, but he'd bet a year's wage that she knew why. "What was in the package?"

"All I saw was a picture of Hersch before he attacked me."

He wondered what else she'd seen. He'd learned a long time ago to trust his instinct, and this time was no different. She wasn't telling him the truth. Not all of it.

Despite how much she had everyone else snowed, a glaring fact took hold of him. The invincible Odie of TES, Cullen's infallible intelligence officer—expert marksman, formidable ex-army operations captain, feared and respected by any and all she encountered—had something to hide.

Chapter 2

Odie considered trying to call Kate Johnson in front of Jag and Cullen. The way Jag kept looking at her changed her mind. He'd already asked too many questions, and his cleverness made her wary. She couldn't tell him about the initials on the package, not until she knew what Kate had discovered.

"So the package contained information about Hersch," Cullen said. "What else was in it to make someone want you dead?"

"I don't know. I didn't get a chance to see everything in the envelope," she answered.

"No, you didn't, did you?" Jag said. "Just one picture, right?"

Odie slid her gaze to him, wanting to shut him up. He was way too suspicious. She could tell by his tone that he didn't believe her.

"Right." She didn't want to tell anyone about the second

photo she'd seen until she found out who the man was and what his connection was to Hersch…and ELF.

"Someone had to have found out about your source," Cullen said.

Kate. Dread fluttered in her middle. Experience told her what to expect but she was still in denial. She tried to cover her worry but was afraid Cullen noticed. Another glance at Jag convinced her he, at least, had.

"Who sent you the information?" Cullen asked.

"You know I never reveal my sources."

"This is an exception. Your source is obviously in danger, if not already dead."

And that was a first for her. Odie caught Jag's deceptively calm scrutiny and had to look out the window. So much was riding on Kate not being dead. She was her most reliable contact. And not just for TES. Now something about ELF had been unearthed and she had a feeling it was not good.

"Odie?"

She turned back to Cullen.

"You know I have to ask," he said.

"I'm sorry, I can't tell you."

His green eyes iced with displeasure that worked to compel most people into confessing everything they knew.

"I'll make sure my contact is all right," she said. "I'll leave tonight."

"To go where?"

She frowned at him in a you-should-know-better way and didn't answer.

"I'm in no mood for your attitude, Odie. If your contact was murdered, this turns into more than spy work. I don't want you to go anywhere alone. Jag will go with you."

"This is one of my best contacts. I have to protect that person. You know how this works, Cullen. Just let me go and make sure everything's all right."

"Have you tried calling this contact?"

"Not yet." She saw that Cullen didn't expect her contact to answer anyway and looked down in consternation.

"Someone tried to kill you, Odie. From now on, you don't go anywhere without Jag."

She raised her gaze. "I don't need any protection." Least of all from a man, doubly not from an adrenaline-pumped special ops dude.

She looked over at Jag. The man was annoying. Too clever. Too good looking. Too tall. Too quiet. Too everything. He had a way of communicating with his eyes, and right now he was telling her that he knew she was keeping something to herself. Yet...he hadn't alerted Cullen.

Why?

"Where is your contact?" Cullen asked.

There was no avoiding revealing that much. She didn't see the harm in that. "Washington, D.C."

"Jag goes with you or you don't go at all."

"All right. Jag can go with me, but we need to leave now. Can you get me a flight tonight?"

"Yes."

"One more thing," Jag said.

And Odie braced herself.

"How did whoever came after you know you went to your contact for information on Hersch?"

How was she supposed to know that? "I don't know." He must be asking for a reason.

"Did you get the package from the same person who sent you the file you briefed me on this morning?"

"Yes." Where was he going with this?

"Did you ask for more information?"

"No."

"So…your contact just sent it to you?"

"Something more must have come up."

"And you have no idea what that might be."

She gave him an unappreciative smirk. "None what-soever." None that she'd reveal. Not yet, anyway. He was just going to have to wait.

"Where might your contact have gotten the new information?" Cullen asked.

"And why was she still looking?" Jag added. "She already gave you what you needed."

"I have no way of knowing that." She told them both with her eyes that she'd answered both of their questions.

"We need to find out," Cullen said.

Odie looked away. It made her sick to think Kate had been exposed because of her. And she'd found something linked to ELF. She resisted the need to put her hand on her churning stomach.

Please, don't let this be as bad as it seems…

"Odie."

She focused on Cullen and saw his genuine concern. "You do know what you're going to find when you get to Washington, don't you?"

She tried to harden herself against the impact of his sobering comment. "Yes…but I'm hoping…I'm hoping…" She hated how unsteady she sounded.

"I'm sorry."

She nodded. Bolstering her willpower, she pushed her softening feelings back and turned to Jag.

"Will you take me home so I can pack and then pick me up when you're ready to go?"

He didn't seem at all affected by her teary show of

emotion. All business and nothing else. "We'll stop by my place first. It won't take me long to pack and I can wait for you to get ready at your place."

So he wasn't going to let her out of his sight. He knew she wanted to go to Washington alone. He also knew she hadn't revealed her reason. Not the entire reason. Since she no longer had a vehicle she couldn't argue.

"All right." But one way or another, she'd find a way to ditch him.

Odie glanced around her as she made her way through Dulles International Airport. Her luck, Jag had gone to Cullen and he'd seen to it that he made it to Washington, D.C., ahead of her. While he'd packed in his bedroom, she'd taken his car keys and after a quick stop at home to pack, she'd driven his Jetta to Denver, where she'd caught a late flight into Dulles. She knew just how bad it would look, but she'd set everything straight as soon as she had answers, no matter how hard those answers were on her.

Finding a taxi, she threw her carry-on onto the backseat and climbed in with her laptop case.

"Grand Hyatt."

Twisting to see behind her, she assured herself that she wasn't being followed. She was safe for now, but it wouldn't be long before Jag caught up to her. She didn't have much time.

She tried Kate's number again, but still there was no answer. Odie relented to the obvious. She tried Kate's father's cell next, but there was no answer there, either. Digging in her laptop case, she found her day-timer and looked up a number for Kate's sister.

Modesty McKenzie answered.

"Mo?" Odie queried.

"Who is this?"

"Odelia Frank." She didn't talk much to Kate's sister, but Mo would remember her.

"Odie. Oh my God. Have you heard?"

Odie closed her eyes. So, it was true. "Can I come see you tonight?"

"Yes. I'm not sleeping anyway. Mom and Dad are on their way back from the Bahamas right now."

That explained why she hadn't been able to get ahold of Senator Raybourne. "I'll be there in about a half hour."

She disconnected as the taxi stopped in front of the hotel. After checking in, she got another cab and gave the driver the address where Kate's sister lived. Her mind was so full of scattered emotions and thoughts that time seemed warped on the way there. Before she knew it the cab stopped.

"Wait for me." She handed the driver two hundred dollar bills.

His eyebrows rose over dark Cuban eyes surrounded by heavy lines and bushy black hair. He reached to take the money. "Take your time."

Odie's unsteady knees threatened her balance as she made her way to the front door, which opened before she reached it. Mo stood there.

Checking to make sure the taxi driver hadn't run off with her money, Odie somberly greeted Mo as she entered the dim, dated home. Low popcorn texture ceilings and off-white walls cast the living room in dreary shadows. Mo shut the door and faced her. In her late-twenties with layered, straight blond hair, her eyes were red and puffy from crying.

"I'm so sorry," Odie said.

Mo came closer and they hugged.

"I'm sorry, too," Mo said. "I know how close you two were."

Odie squeezed her eyes shut as tears sprouted. She and Kate had known each other all their lives. She leaned back from Mo.

"When my mother told me I was so shocked," Mo said. "It's the strangest thing. Someone tells you your sister was murdered and it doesn't seem real."

Shock didn't begin to come close to describing the chaos taking place inside Odie. More than losing a good friend, this could expose something very dangerous. Kate had been trying to help her, and now Kate was dead.

"What happened?" Odie asked.

"The police don't know much. They say there was no evidence from the scene that gives them any leads. No witnesses, either. She fought hard. There were signs of a violent struggle…before her throat was slit."

Odie raked her fingers through her hair, pulling back dark strands that had fallen too close to her face.

Kate. Oh God…why did it have to be Kate?

"Did she say anything to you? Was she worried about anything or seem anxious?" she asked.

"No. I haven't seen her in over a week."

"Did she mention talking to anyone? Seeing anyone?"

"No, and she never talked about her work."

"Who found her?"

"Her boyfriend. He was living with her, but he wasn't home when it happened. The police have already questioned him. They haven't named him as a suspect, but he's still under investigation."

Finally. A lead. "What's his name?"

"Calan Friese." She spelled the name for her. "He's

ex-Delta. Just your kind of guy." She smiled a little but the sorrow never left her eyes.

"How did they meet?"

"A mutual friend had a barbecue."

"Who was the mutual friend?"

"Kate didn't say. All she said was that they both knew a colonel who had a barbecue."

Odie nodded. That might be worth looking into.

"Dad's taking it pretty hard," Mo said.

Odie could only imagine. Luis Raybourne was Kate's stepfather and the only father she'd ever known. Mo was his flesh-and-blood daughter, but she'd never had a taste for politics so their relationship was different than the one he had with Kate. He loved both his girls, but Mo was a wife and mother and Kate was an outspoken political dynamo. Luis had a seat on the Senate Arms Services Committee. He and Kate had never run out of things to talk about. Her death had to be devastating for him.

"He'll be glad to see you," Mo added. "I'll let you know when the funeral is."

"I wish it was under different circumstances." Luis and Odie's father had met in the army when she and Kate were just kids, but after Sage and her father died, she'd lost touch with him.

As for Calan Friese, she'd learn his background before she went to see him. She always liked to know the person she wanted to question, or have one of TES's operatives question for her. It sometimes gave her leverage. She could use any vulnerabilities she found in her background investigations to her advantage. Friese would be at the funeral, too. She'd get a good look at him to start with. Get to know his body language. See if he was anxious.

"How did you find out?" Mo asked.

Odie hesitated, not sure how much she should say. She didn't want to give Mo false hope, not before she had something solid to go on, and she didn't want to put her life in danger by telling her things she didn't need to know.

"She wasn't answering her phone," Odie answered. "I got worried." She hoped Mo wouldn't question her further.

"When did you last talk to her?"

Not since she'd sent that first package of information about defense initiatives, but if she told Mo that, it might provoke her curiosity. "I don't know. A few days ago," she lied.

"And she seemed normal?"

"Yes." Keep it short, she told herself. Mo wasn't in the same league as she and Kate were. She could be misled, and for her sake, Odie would do just that.

She saw how Mo contemplated the way she'd answered. "You flew all the way here just because she wasn't answering her phone?"

Crap.

"It isn't like her not to answer her phone. Besides, I had other business here. I just bumped up my schedule." It wasn't a total lie....

The curiosity smoothed from Mo's expression and now she just looked sad. Time to say goodbye before she started questioning her again.

"Try and get some sleep," she said. "I'll see you at the funeral."

"Thanks for coming."

Odie left, already planning on how she'd go about getting information on Calan Friese. And how to face Jag. He was bound to be in D.C. by now.

Odie entered the hotel, which opened to a wide expanse of trees and plants beneath a towering atrium flanked by several floors of balconies. On the far side she could barely see the checkout counter. She moved her gaze back to a sofa surrounded by chairs and tables and lots of vegetation and spotted him.

Jag unfolded his big frame from the chair where he'd sat waiting for her. She stopped walking as he approached. His legs were long in dark blue jeans and the black boots made him look tough. So did the black T-shirt. Never mind that. She'd expected this, for him to find her and for it not to take long, but seeing him was jarring. Why did she feel this sudden rush of attraction?

"Get what you needed?" he asked, his eyes giving nothing away. Was he angry? Did he have to hide a reciprocating attraction?

"My contact is dead." She kept her emotion out of it.

"I know," he said.

How did he know? She waited for him to tell her.

"Cullen called someone he knew," he explained as if she'd asked aloud. "Kate Johnson?"

Odie folded her arms. Damn that Cullen. He knew too much about how she operated.

"Was a senior analyst for the CIA, working Middle East issues." He nodded as though impressed. "I'm almost afraid to ask how you landed such a valuable contact."

"She was my friend."

"It's too late to protect her, so why don't you tell me what you think was in that package?"

Lowering her arms, she brushed past him and marched toward the elevators, stabbing the Up button with her forefinger as he came to a stop next to her.

"You do realize how guilty you're making yourself appear?"

She didn't look at him. "I didn't see what was in the package."

"But you have an idea what was."

She didn't answer right away. "I didn't see enough to tell." It was true enough.

"You saw something."

"You guys are all the same. Always asking endless questions and jumping to conclusions."

"The right conclusions."

She glowered at him, too aware of his big, fit body.

"Why do you hate men who do special ops so much?"

The elevator doors opened and she stepped inside, ignoring him as she pressed the floor button.

"Cullen told me about your first husband," he said.

A too-familiar pang gripped her chest. "When did he tell you that?" The doors closed and the elevator began to move.

"After I told him you went to D.C. without me."

Why had he told Jag that?

"He noticed your odd behavior, too."

"This has nothing to do with Sage."

"Sage?"

She used her eyes to warn him not to push her too far.

"I asked him the same question I just asked you."

"If you already know the answer, why ask me?"

"I wanted to see what you'd say."

Great, here we go. He was going to pry now. She watched the numbers climb as the elevator rose. "Cullen should learn to keep his mouth shut."

"It must have been hard, losing him that way."

"He was shot in the line of duty. Doing what he loved."

"I can understand why you put such a high wall up for the men you get involved with."

She faced him. "Look, you don't know me. And I'm not in the mood to talk about this with you."

"Not all of them die," he said anyway.

She folded her arms, feeling a lump of sorrow clog her throat. It had been six years and still she hadn't gotten past the hurt. The what-ifs…

"No wonder you're so good at what you do."

The elevator stopped. "What's that supposed to mean?"

"You have a strong sense of purpose. Losing the man you loved. Was he fighting terrorists?"

He followed her into the hall. "You are such a bastard." Was he deliberately trying to catch her vulnerable or did he wonder if her secret had something to do with her ex?

"What? I'm expressing sympathy."

"You're fishing. You're trying to get me to talk."

"Why don't you?"

At her room. She opened the door and stepped inside, meaning to close the door but Jag pushed it open and came into the room, forcing her to back up. He let the door shut.

"Get your own room," she said.

He looked toward the two queen beds. "This'll do just fine."

Just imagining him staying the night was almost frightening. "I've told you all I know about what was in the package." And that was the truth. She didn't know the man in the photo.

He must have recognized that as he watched her face. His eyes softened with satisfaction, at least for the moment.

"We need to work together on this. Are you going to be able to do that?"

"Of course." Unless it was related to ELF.

"You'll share whatever you find?"

"Yes." Unless it was related to ELF.

"Who did you go see tonight?"

That she could answer. "Kate's sister."

"What did she say?"

"Nothing, which doesn't surprise me. Kate never involved friends and family in her work."

"How do you know her death was related to her work?"

"I don't."

"I thought she was just helping you. You know, on the side as it were, since she already had a good enough job."

"She was."

He sighed at her evasiveness. "Will there be someone at her funeral we can talk to?"

"You don't have to go to her funeral with me."

He cocked his head at her lame attempt to get him to leave her alone. "It's no trouble."

No trouble. Not for him. What was she going to do with him hanging around all the time? Nothing, that's what. She'd wait for the funeral—see who showed up—and then she'd go from there.

Now her only concern was getting through the next couple of days alone with him.

It was sunny and warm the day of Kate's funeral. Standing near the casket as the minister finished his eulogy, Odie watched the mourners. She knew Jag was doing the same beside her, tall and big and handsome and way too distracting. He didn't know these people the way she did, but she didn't doubt he'd notice things—like the man standing next to Senator Raybourne and his wife and daughter. It had to be Calan Friese. Odie was already suspicious of him. He showed no emotion and yet his long-term girlfriend had just been murdered.

She sneaked a glance at Jag. Yep, he'd noticed. Just as his head started to turn toward her, she faced forward and tried to pay attention to the service.

The past two days had been a challenge. She'd barely managed to maintain her aloofness sharing meals and a room with a man who attracted her against her will. The only thing that saved her was her laptop. She had used the excuse of working to keep her distance. But like the trained operative he was, he'd endured the boredom with style. She'd even caught him amused while he observed her.

The minister approached the senator and his wife. Odie hadn't seen them in a long time. Luis looked different, still tall but his middle was beginning to protrude and his hair was gray. Alice began crying uncontrollably and he put his arm around her. She wasn't gray but she probably dyed her hair. Slender and stylish in her long black dress, she looked fabulous. For an older woman, she sure knew how to keep her shape. Mo stood next to them, mouth tight with the effort not to cry. Luis put his other arm around her, a stoic rock of support for his family.

She wondered if he could help her. As a senator, he could have valuable connections. Maybe it would lead to something.

Something linked to Hersch, a voice taunted in her mind. She felt a disturbing chill run down her back. How deep did this go? Cullen also had connections in the government, and at least one of them had asked him to carry out this mission. But what had triggered the inquiry into Defense Initiatives? Who had tipped off Cullen's higher-ups to the Albanian company?

She moved her focus again to Friese. Tall and expressionless, he had dark blond hair and wore sunglasses. To hide his lack of tears? He was on the thick side with muscle. No fat. He had all the signs of special ops.

Feeling Jag watching her, she looked up at him. Without even trying to pretend he hadn't noticed where her gaze had gone, he looked away.

Mourners began to line up to offer their condolences to Kate's family. It wasn't easy to watch. Odie waited until the last of them finished before leading Jag there.

"You didn't tell me Kate's father was a senator."

"I thought you already knew."

"I had to read about it."

"Poor baby."

"What else am I going to read about?"

She glanced at him as they approached Luis and his family. "Don't embarrass me."

He grunted a laugh. "Is that even possible?"

"Odelia," Luis said, reaching out his arms. She went into them and they hugged.

"Your mom couldn't make it?" he asked as he leaned back.

Odie shook her head. "She's in Egypt right now."

"She's still traveling all over the world?"

The reason why gave her a pang of sadness. "Yes, ever since Dad died." She and her mother had that in common. They'd both lost their husbands. It made for sad reunions, which is why they hadn't had many in the years since.

Odie hugged Mo. "If there's anything I can do, just call."

"Thanks." Mo braved a small smile before turning to the next mourner.

Odie moved on to Alice. She didn't even try to say anything to the woman. What words were there for a mother who'd lost a daughter?

"Thank you for coming," Alice managed to say. It sounded feeble.

"Of course," Odie said, looking at Luis.

His kind eyes showed how much his grief ravaged him.

"I'm so sorry," she said to Alice.

"You were close to her, too."

"Yes."

"You were her best friend." Alice dabbed her eyes with a tissue.

Luis's eyes misted as he watched his wife. When he finally managed to control his emotions, he cleared his throat and turned to Odie again.

"Kate told me you were getting married." He looked pointedly at Jag, the change in subject pushing the grief from his eyes. "I was sorry I had to miss the wedding."

He must have been in the Bahamas when her wedding had fallen to disaster and her wedding had been small. He and Alice hadn't been there. Wait a minute… Did he think…

A flash of astonishment stunned her for a second. He thought she was with Jag…like *that?* "This isn't my husband." *Oh, my God.* "This is Jag Benney. He works at TES."

"Ah. Then he couldn't be your husband." He chuckled and turned to Jag. "She has an aversion to special forces types."

"Yeah, I picked up on that the first time I met her."

Odie slid a look at him. Had he? Most newbies who walked through TES doors checked her out without holding back. Jag had shown no emotion. It had impressed her, though she'd never tell him that.

"Where is your husband?" Luis asked Odie. "Is he here?" He glanced around.

"I didn't get married." She did not want to explain it again. "We canceled."

"You can add engineers to her list of not eligible," Jag said, clearly enjoying her stiffening mood.

She bit back a sarcastic retort.

"Well, I'm sorry to hear that, Odie," Luis said, then again turned to Jag. "I've always told her there's only one kind of man for her, and it's the kind that Cullen employs. They're the only ones who have half a chance of standing up to her."

Jag chuckled, a low, deep sound. "I never thought of it that way, but you're probably right." He grinned at Odie.

Damn him.

Seeing Mo and her mother move away from the senator to join a couple and their teenaged daughter, who greeted them in typical funeral-mode fashion, Odie used the appearance of distraction to ignore both of them.

"Well, if you aren't married to this fellow, why is he here? Are you working?" Luis asked.

"Not at the moment," Jag said, no longer sounding amused. Clearly their work was a subject he didn't want broached.

Luis looked at her, a silent question in his eyes. If they weren't working why was Jag at Kate's funeral with her? He knew how much losing her husband had hurt her and how she felt about dating operatives.

"Our assignment was waylaid after we heard of Kate's murder."

"Ah." He nodded. "How long will you be in D.C.?"

"I'm not sure. It depends on how long it takes to find Kate's killer." If they ever did.

"I went to Langley and asked around," Luis said.

Odie perked up with interest.

"No one could help. Her death doesn't appear to be connected to her job."

No, because it was connected to Hersch...or more precisely, ELF.

"What about her boyfriend?" Odie caught the way Jag turned to look at her. She hadn't told him about Calan.

Luis nodded. "I wanted to talk to you about that. I checked him out. He doesn't have a solid alibi the night of Kate's murder. The police have questioned him and I don't think they've ruled him out as a suspect, but there's no evidence implicating him. No prints. And no motive, at least, not yet."

That was essentially what Mo had said. "Did you talk to him?"

"I haven't had the chance. Here at the funeral..."

Friese had stood right next to him but, yes, it might have gotten ugly at Kate's funeral if Luis had started asking questions.

"I was going to go see him tomorrow, but now that you're here..."

"I'll take care of it."

"*We'll* take care of it," Jag corrected.

Odie wanted to roll her eyes.

Luis chuckled. "You'll have to get used to Odie's independence. She's a little more high-strung than most other women. She likes to do things her way."

Jag grunted. "Well, I like to do things my way, too, so we have something in common." He smiled cheekily at her.

Meaning, he'd get his way and stick to her like duct tape.

Luis missed the exchange and said, "I brought you everything I have on him. It's in my car."

"Great. That's wonderful." A burst of hope encouraged her.

"What have you gotten so far?"

"Not much, I'm afraid." Careful not to look at Jag, knowing he wouldn't want her to say anything, she added, "But I did receive a package from Kate a few days ago."

"Odie," Jag warned. "The details of this assignment are confidential," he told Luis.

"Your assignment is related to Kate?"

"No," Jag said before Odie could answer.

"It's all right," Luis said, catching on. "I understand the way these things operate."

"I didn't get a chance to see everything that was in the package," Odie said despite Jag's presence. "Just a picture of a man TES is investigating."

"Odie, that's enough."

"What do you mean you didn't get a chance?" Luis asked.

She ignored Jag's rising temper. "Someone tried to kill me."

"What—"

"A man broke into my house. He was after the package." She told him about her kidnapping and what had followed.

"Where is the package? Do you have it?"

"No. It burned with my truck."

"My Lord. Are you sure you're all right?" He gestured to the mark on her cheek. "I was wondering where you got that."

"I'm fine. Jag rescued me in the nick of time." She sent Jag an exaggerated glance. "Hero that he is."

He cocked his head in annoyance.

"Who was in the picture?" Luis asked.

Jag turned to him. "We can't tell you that."

Odie narrowed her eyes at him, but he didn't acknowledge her. She faced Luis. "When's the last time you talked to Kate?"

"I saw her about a week before she was killed, and she didn't say anything unusual, nor did I think she was afraid of anything. That was the last time I had contact with her." He fell into a sad moment.

"Did she ask you for any information? Anything on anyone in particular?"

"Like who? The man TES is investigating?"

The man in the photo Odie had seen.

"We should get going," Jag said, and she knew he'd had enough.

"She didn't," Luis said to Odie. "I'll bring what I have on Friese to the reception."

"Okay, see you in a while."

He waved and started toward the remaining parked vehicles.

Odie looked for Calan Friese but didn't see him.

"He already left for the reception," Jag told her.

Did he never stop observing? He must have listened to her conversation with Luis and kept vigil at the same time.

She walked toward the car with him. A man on a motorcycle caught her eye. He wore jeans and a black leather jacket and the helmet on his head made it hard to see much of his face. None of his hair peeked out from the helmet. Though he wore sunglasses, he seemed to be looking right at them. Had he been among the crowd at the funeral? She didn't think so. As they drew nearer, he started the bike.

"Do you see that?" she asked Jag without looking at him.

"Yeah. No plate on the front."

The man rode down the cemetery lane and Odie saw that the rear plate was missing, too. Whoever he was, he didn't seem to want anyone here to be able to identify him.

Why not?

Chapter 3

Jag left Odie sleeping in the room before driving to Mo McKenzie's house. He fully expected her to disappear while he was gone. The way she'd avoided telling him about Friese had cued him plenty. But he'd seen her checking out the guy standing next to Senator Raybourne. Kate's boyfriend. While she'd been talking to the senator, he'd seen the man leave the funeral and get into a white truck.

Jag pulled his rental car to a stop in front of Mo's house. About the time he finished here, Odie would probably be on the move. The senator had given her a file folder yesterday just as he'd promised, and she hadn't shared its contents with him. That grated on him. But the modified GPS transmitter in her purse, which was more of a work tote—Odie wasn't a purse type of woman—would tell him all he needed for now.

Stepping to Mo's front door, he knocked, glancing

around while he waited. No one on the street. No cars passed. No one peered through windows.

The door opened and an attractive blonde eyed him through the space allowed by the security bar. Her brow lowered warily.

"Mo McKenzie?" he queried, even though he knew it was her.

"Who are you?"

"Jag Benney. I work with Odelia Frank. I was with her at the funeral."

Her wariness smoothed and she unlocked the door. Opening it, she looked curiously past him. "Where is Odie?"

"She isn't here. Do you mind if I ask you a few questions?"

"Without Odie?"

"Actually, it's Odie I need to talk to you about."

Her perplexity showed. "Why?"

"I know she came to see you, but did she tell you someone tried to kill her?"

The abruptness of it caused Mo a moment of stunned silence. "What? No. What happened?"

He'd answer that in a minute. "Did she tell you about a package Kate sent her?"

Confusion ravaged Mo's expression. "No," she said unsteadily. "When did Kate send her a package? What was in it?"

Just as he'd hoped, Odie hadn't told the woman anything. She was too protective of her secret. It was the carrot he'd hoped she would leave for him to dangle.

Mo opened the door wider, allowing him to enter.

Stepping inside, Jag faced her in the entry. "Odie claims she didn't have time to see the contents of the package before someone attacked her in her house," he said, and explained everything, leaving out Odie's strange behavior and the connection to Hersch. As Odie had probably intended, he didn't want to put Mo in danger.

"Is that why Kate was killed?" Mo asked. "Because she discovered something?"

"That's what I'm going to find out."

"Does Odie know more than she's letting on?"

He hesitated, not wanting to hurt her at a time like this. "I'm afraid of that, yes."

"But…why would she do that? Why would she withhold information that might lead us to the person who killed Kate?"

Jag didn't know, and it was enough to let Mo fill in her own blanks. He watched her face map out emotions of worry and hurt. Odie was supposed to be a friend and she might be working against the people closest to her.

"What do you need to know?" she finally asked.

"How much do you know about what she does?"

"Not much. I know she works for someone named Cullen McQueen."

"She did special ops before she went to work for him, didn't she?"

"Yes. She was an operations captain with the army. Mostly Middle East issues. Why?"

He knew that, but it was a soft way to lead into his next question. "Why did she leave? It seems like she was on her way to a successful career."

"Odie is a very driven woman. I think part of her got bored and wanted something new and maybe a little more challenging."

"That wasn't challenging enough?" It didn't mesh.

"Well…there was the matter of her husband dying. She resigned shortly after that and then Cullen found her."

Jag had an idea what it was like to love someone that much. While his wife hadn't died, she may as well have. His idea of her certainly had. And that's what he mourned more than anything.

"What got her into counterterror ops?" he asked.

"Her dad was a colonel who ran counterterror operations. She always admired him. Daddy's little girl, you know? I think she wanted to follow in his footsteps in some way. She was doing that with the army, and she's continuing it now, with that secret company she works for."

"Where is her father now?"

"He died. Five years ago."

A year after her husband died. She'd had two hard blows.

"He was murdered."

That stopped him short. "What happened?"

"Nobody really knows. His killer was never caught. But Odie thinks it was a professional hit."

What the hell...? "Why does she think that?"

"He was shot twice in the head and there was no sign of a struggle."

"Were there any leads?"

She shook her head. "The crime scene was too clean and Odie's dad was well respected. Who would want to kill him? Not even Odie knew the answer to that. It was hard on her. Still is."

"You're telling me that in five years nothing's come up?"

"Not that I know of."

"Odie hasn't found anything? Nothing?" *That* he had a hard time believing. Her secretiveness only convinced him more. She knew something. She just wasn't telling anyone. Why?

"No."

"Don't you think that's strange? Someone with Odie's background should be able to learn something."

"Whoever killed her dad must have covered his tracks extremely well."

"I'd say." Or she'd covered hers. But why? What was the need for secrets? Her father was murdered. Unless he was involved in something outside the law. Would Odie go to extremes to hide that?

"What was her father working on when he was killed? What was he doing?" he asked.

"I don't know. Odie never told me. What reason would she have to say anything? She doesn't operate that way."

True.

"What was his name?"

"Edward Leland Ferguson."

He made a mental note of that so he could do a little of his own digging later. "How did she get on with TES?"

"Her father knew someone who got in touch with the man who runs it."

"Who did he know?"

"I don't know. Odie's work is always so clandestine. I never ask about it and she never volunteers information. All I know is going to work for that company was the best thing that could have happened to her after her husband died. Everyone was pretty worried about her, especially her father. It was good to see her bounce back."

Jag nodded. Odie had had a good relationship with her father, and he'd had a stellar reputation. But what had he been involved in and why hadn't Odie said anything about it?

"I just can't imagine Odie deliberately hindering Kate's murder investigation," Mo said.

Yes, it was out of character for her. She was tenacious in her counterterrorism work. Righteous and thorough. "If she is, I don't think it's because she means to. I think she's afraid of something."

"Odie?"

Jag nodded. Odie wasn't afraid of anything, and the fact that she was now convinced him she was in danger. Big danger.

"Someone tried to kill her, remember," Jag said.

With a grave and thoughtful nod, Mo stared off into her living room.

"Don't worry, I'll make sure she's all right," Jag said. He didn't want to give her more burden than she already had.

"But…what if whatever she's hiding is…wrong?"

"We'll hope for the best. We'll hope she's just scared and doesn't want to ask for help."

A tiny smile of appreciation made its way to her grief-lined mouth. "You're someone she can trust. I can tell."

He wanted her to trust him, but that didn't mean he'd trust her. Dishonesty went against his grain. He couldn't tolerate it, not after the way his marriage had ended. He'd turn Odie in without a second thought if she was doing something she shouldn't.

"You care about her." It was more of a statement than a question.

It caught him off guard.

"I can tell," she said again.

What could she tell? He couldn't deny he'd been interested in Odie the first time he'd met her, but she wasn't interested in him. And she wasn't being straight with him.

"It won't be good for anyone if I'm wrong." And that was all he'd say on the matter.

Her smile warmed. "I don't think you are."

He sure hoped so. "Thank you, Mo."

"No, thank you. I was worried about Odie before but I'm not now."

Time to go. He wasn't comfortable with her insight—romantic and maybe a little too accurate.

Odie paid the taxi driver and stepped onto the sidewalk in front of a Mexican chain restaurant. She paused to stare above the building's roofline at the Marilyn Monroe painting on the side of the hair salon next door. Searching the street, she saw no sign of Jag, but she knew he wouldn't be far behind. She almost smiled. Did he really think she was stupid enough not to find the transmitter he'd slipped into her work tote? She'd indulged him by leaving it there, and took her tote with her—which she wouldn't have done otherwise. The bag was just one more thing to carry if she had to leave in a hurry.

A white Lexus pulled into a parking space not far down the street, but the driver didn't get out. Was he looking at her? She'd check to see if he was still there when she finished with Calan Friese. She needed all her wits for this one.

The information Luis had given her more than explained why the police hadn't eliminated him as a suspect. Not only were his whereabouts the night of Kate's murder sketchy, he'd had a wife whose throat had been slit seven years ago. The killer had never been found. Kate's throat had been slit. And like his wife's murder, there was no evidence pointing to the killer.

Odie thought of the initials on the package Kate had sent. Was Calan somehow connected?

It made her wonder why he'd agreed to meet her. Was

he so sure of his innocence or did he want to find out what she knew?

She entered the restaurant. A quick look around confirmed Calan wasn't there yet.

Finding a table in the semi-crowded space, she hung her work tote over the back of the chair and sat facing the front entrance, listening to the noise of conversation bouncing off the high ceiling and corrugated aluminum siding. Just two or three minutes later she saw him walk along the sidewalk. He opened the door and entered, seeing her almost immediately. He didn't smile. Not wearing sunglasses, she saw that his eyes were blue. He was an attractive man, not pretty or fair like some blond-haired, blue-eyed men. He was more rugged than that. But didn't they all have that look? That special ops, he-man look that she'd grown to dislike so much. Except this man wasn't a hero if he'd murdered his wife and then later on a girlfriend.

"Sorry I didn't get a chance to meet you at the funeral," he said, pulling out the chair across from her.

"Did you want to?" she asked, nonchalant…and then… not.

He sat, his eyes unwavering and not missing her taunt. "Kate told me about you."

"Really? What did she say?"

"That you're a ball-breaker and you work for a mountaineering company in Colorado."

"Accurate enough." She wasn't going to play down his perception. Kate had told him what she was supposed to tell everyone. Minus the ball-breaker part.

"RC Mountaineering," he said. "Run by none other than Cullen McQueen."

She supposed it wouldn't be too hard to find that out.

"What do you do for him?"

Did he really think she'd tell him? "I'm the cashier."

That pulled a cynical laugh from him.

"Where were you the night Kate was killed?" She didn't waste time asking.

"I went for a drive." He sounded belligerent.

"Is that the truth?"

"It's what I told the police."

Cocky bastard. "Did anyone see you? Can you prove it?"

"No."

She searched his face and found nothing that showed his emotion. Of course, his background made these games easy for him, and the dangerous edge surrounding him fit the caricature of so many that Cullen employed. Regardless of her bias, Odie didn't like to see those traits used for the wrong reason.

"Did you kill her?" she asked.

He leaned comfortably back in his chair, appearing to enjoy this. "What reason would I have to kill my girlfriend? Wouldn't it be easier to just break up with her?"

"I don't know, would it?"

He didn't respond.

"Did you know what she was working on?"

"I didn't kill her," he said. His eyes never changed, but his lack of response to her question made her wonder if he did know what Kate was working on.

"What did she uncover?"

"You think she uncovered something?"

Odie sighed, getting impatient. "You know I do. And I know you know something, so why don't we just cut the bull and come clean?"

"Okay, you first."

Odie didn't like his smart mouth. "Did you kill your wife seven years ago?"

Now his eyes changed, a subtle flinch, but it was there. "That subject is off-limits."

Why? Because he was guilty or was he still upset about his loss? "Don't you find it peculiar that both their throats were slit?"

"I would think a woman like you would have already checked the police record."

"I didn't have time."

He just met her gaze with cold indifference. He knew she'd checked the report, but he wasn't going to budge.

Fine. "Where were you going on your *drive?* You don't really expect anyone to believe that, do you?"

"Nowhere in particular," he replied, ignoring the rest of what she'd said. But he sounded annoyed. And emotion had put it there. Emotion over his girlfriend's death, and his wife's before that. Interesting. Crime of passion or unresolved grief?

"Why were you driving?"

"I needed some time alone."

"Why?"

Leaning forward with his elbows on the table, he said, "I had an argument with Kate."

Was he taunting her? She leaned on the table, too, imitating him. "About what?"

"A woman like you has a lot of resources working for someone like McQueen," he said.

She found the comment a little strange. "You know him?"

"Never met him. I've heard of him, though."

"What's your point?"

He smirked and rose to his feet. "Have a nice day."

Did her association with TES make him nervous? Well, it should.

"Does the name Nigel Hersch mean anything to you?" she put out there for him.

He stilled just as she'd expected and then faced her beside the table, the blue of his fearless eyes streaming out between thick lashes.

When the silence stretched too long, she asked, "How much did Kate tell you about him?"

"How much did she tell you?"

She wasn't going to tell him a thing if he wasn't going to reciprocate. "What about Edward Ferguson? Ever heard of him?"

He shrugged and shook his head, noncommittal.

Odie had to force herself not to react. He knew. Why was he playing cat and mouse? Edward was her father. She would like nothing more than to catch his killer. And now Kate's. Whose side was Friese on? Hers or his own? And why had he agreed to meet her? Was it really only to fish for information? To find out what she knew? Maybe now he wasn't worried. She didn't know enough.

"Did you love Kate?" she asked.

Emotion ravaged his eyes for a second or two. Strong emotion. Pushing its way to the surface, past his soldier's armor.

"Good luck with your investigation," he said, and walked toward the short line in front of the concession counter. He was going to get something to eat, as if their conversation hadn't meant a thing. Only it had. It had been written all over his face.

Did he love Kate or hate her enough to kill her like his wife? Odie debated on whether to wait and continue to talk to him or take his dismissal and go. He wasn't going to tell her anything. The fact that he'd done his homework and had pieced together where she worked convinced her. Surely he knew what she was capable of with TES behind her. If he was innocent, he could trust her. But he didn't. And that could only mean he was playing his own side, not hers or anyone else's. Guilty. He had something to hide. Was it murder? Was it the contents of Kate's package? Both?

She stood and left the restaurant. Outside, she spotted Jag leaning against his rental car. Sunglasses on, light brown hair messy, arms folded, legs crossed at the ankles. His biceps bulged in a short-sleeved dark green golf shirt and his lean thighs cupped his groin. Without even trying, the man did sexy like a Chinese fireworks explosion.

She stopped in front of him, smiling and unable to subdue the spark of excitement over seeing him. She caught him looking her over, too, saw the way his head moved down a little and then back up. She was in a white cotton T-shirt and white-washed jeans with Gore-Tex leather hiking boots. Nothing sexy about it, but he made her feel like she was in a little black dress.

"Get what you needed?" he asked with a hint of amusement.

"How did you know I was here?" she asked, even though she already knew.

"Lucky guess." He pushed off the car, straightening his tall frame. "You know, you're going to have to start trusting me."

Odie reached into her tote and pulled out the GPS device and handed it to him. He opened his palm for her to drop it there.

She tipped her head back, putting her face close to his. "I do trust you."

A grin spread over his mouth, showing off straight,

white teeth and putting creases around his eyes. He really had to stop with the sex appeal thing.

"Every time I think I have you figured out, you do something like this," he said.

"Good." She liked his straightforwardness and the way his ego wasn't injured that she'd outsmarted him. Trying to cover her warming appreciation, she looked toward the spot where she'd seen the Lexus park. It was still there, driver behind the wheel. Not very good at surveillance.

"Who is that?" Jag asked.

"Don't know, but he's no professional."

"I noticed. Want to see if we can get him to play?" He opened the passenger door for her.

Smiling back at him, she said, "Sure," and got in.

Chapter 4

"Who'd you meet at the restaurant?" Jag asked as he drove. "The guy from the funeral?"

"Yes," Odie told him easily. She knew it wouldn't take him long to get to this. "Calan Friese."

He seemed pleased that she'd told him. "What do you know about him?"

She hadn't shown him the file Luis had given her and he hadn't pressed her to. That both impressed and worried her. He'd given her the space she needed, but he was also confident enough to either learn what he needed on his own or take his time prying it out of her.

"An aimless ex-Delta, from what I can tell. Kept odd jobs on and off over the last few years. Ever since his wife was murdered. Throat was slit just like Kate's."

"Any motive?"

"Nothing that came up in the reports. For Kate, either." She waited while he digested that.

"Did you make any headway when you talked to him?" he finally asked.

"No. He didn't give an inch."

He glanced over at her, searching her face for a few seconds before turning toward the windshield again. He didn't believe her.

"He didn't tell me anything," she assured him. "He was good. He even knew about Cullen."

"Why'd he meet you?"

"He was feeling me out."

"Lucky guy."

That made her laugh briefly. "Ha, ha. That's funny."

He pulled into a parking space along U Street.

Odie looked around. "Where are we?"

"I'm hungry." He looked in the rearview mirror. "Let's see if our friend is, too."

She was hungry, too. She got out and walked beside him down the sidewalk, seeing the Lexus pass along the street. He wore a hat and a jean jacket with the collar up. Another car passed, blocking their view.

"I can't see the plate number," Jag said.

"Me, either." The Lexus was too far away now.

Two blocks later she spotted Jag's intended destination, a narrow white-and-red building accentuated by a bold sign. Jag opened the door for her and she followed to the end of a moderate line of people. The 1950s décor looked original.

"I've always wanted to try this place." She took in the booths and red stools with shiny metal frames.

"I come here every time I'm in town." He kept looking out the front window for the Lexus.

"He'll be easy enough to spot when we leave," she said.

And Jag nodded. "That's for sure."

She started reading the menu above the busy staff behind the long diner counter. The kitchen looked well used for the better part of a half century and the staff wore T-shirts and jeans with dirty aprons that said *The Spicy Bowl*.

"Not much of a fancy eater, are you?" she said, liking that about him.

"I can lift my pinky with the best of them, but I highly recommend the chili smother."

She read that menu item. "Yummy, but fattening."

"You're concerned about fat?"

"A girl has to watch her figure." Was she flirting with him? It was so easy. She eyed him, bewildered that he could do that to her.

"You don't need to worry about counting calories."

"You should see what happens to my butt when I don't."

"It's a nice butt. Hard to do much damage to that."

The woman in front of them turned to look at them, facing forward when Odie caught her.

"Why, thank you," she said to Jag. She'd forget he was an operative for today.

Watching the workers behind the counter whip up chili concoctions, surrounded by people in the tiny café, Odie sighed and tipped her head back, smelling the aroma. "I miss Washington so much."

"Roaring Creek doesn't seem like your kind of town."

Looking back and up at him, her head still angled, she wondered why all the operatives had to be so damn good-looking. "It isn't. But Cullen fell in love with a mountain girl."

"I thought it was strange a woman like you worked there."

"What do you mean, a woman like me?" She didn't think

he'd noticed much about her. Not as a woman, especially one he might be interested in.

"Until I saw how much you respect Cullen."

She checked to make sure no one was listening to this. The woman in front of them was ordering.

"Don't get sappy on me." She did not want to talk about her loyalty to Cullen. There was a reason for her loyalty, and she didn't want the conversation to go there.

"Maybe there's hope for you after all," he said.

"Sappy…"

"You're unapproachable to anyone other than Cullen. Maybe you can learn something from him."

She spoke her mind and didn't gloss over the truth. Did that make her unapproachable? To operatives, yes. Cullen was different. He was her friend.

"Scared you off, didn't I?" She kept it light. Anything to steer him clear of what had made her unapproachable.

"No, I've just learned to recognize the signs when a woman isn't interested."

That gave her pause. "You were interested? How could I have missed that? I never miss that."

"I could tell. You were defensive."

"I was not."

"I think that's why you come on so strong," he said, confirming what she thought he'd seen in her and touching her at the same time. No one had ever noticed so much about her. "You scare them off before they have a chance to give it their best shot."

She couldn't even argue with him. She'd already teased him about scaring him off. "I was interested." She said it before she realized what she was revealing to him.

Sensing his look, she didn't turn to meet it. The woman ahead of them finished ordering. They were next.

"Two Reds," Jag told the black man behind the counter.

Odie let him buy hers.

Taking their food, Jag led her to two vacant stools at the other end of the counter. She sat next to him and used a fork to take her first bite of the chili-laden sausage. Spicy chili and mustard and onions melted in her mouth.

"Mmm." She closed her eyes and savored the taste.

"You didn't seem interested."

She stopped chewing to look at him.

"You didn't think I was going to let that one go, did you?"

She couldn't tell if he was flirting or leading up to something. "Just because I was interested doesn't mean it would be good for me to explore it." She wished she hadn't let that slip.

"You do seem to keep a lot bottled up."

What did he mean by that? Whatever he said next was what he really wanted to say.

"There are things about you that I doubt even Cullen knows."

She stopped chewing another bite. Oh, he was so smooth. She was going to have to watch out for him from now on. "Like what?"

"Things you keep to yourself."

He was using this nice time they were having together as a way of cracking her. All the enjoyment of flirting with him drained away. "Everyone doesn't need to know personal details about me. I'm not an open book. So what?"

He didn't seem to like that. His eyes hardened and no

longer sparkled with amusement. "Did Kate find something on your father's murder?" he asked. "Is that what you're hiding?"

How the hell had he surmised that? "I'm not hiding anything."

"Is that a no?"

"What do you know about my father's murder?" she countered.

"Probably nothing close to what you know."

"What's that supposed to mean?"

"Five years is a long time for someone like you not to uncover something. Surely you've discovered something since then."

She didn't respond. What could she say that wouldn't make her seem shady and dishonest? Nothing. Working for a man like Cullen, there was no room for that. Cullen would not understand. And neither would Jag. None of them would. She needed more facts, that's all. Once she had them, then she could explain.

That nagging sense that maybe she was wrong threatened her usual aplomb like it always did when she thought too long on it. What if her father wasn't as innocent as she'd always believed? She'd have to reveal what she knew, and what she'd withheld.

"What did you find out about your father's gambling debt?" Jag asked, jarring her back to the present.

"How did you find out about that?"

"I read an old news article."

An article that had speculated her father had been killed for nonpayment, but that wasn't true. The police had confirmed it. "He didn't gamble. That was a rumor started by a reporter who saw him in Vegas." And she wondered if it had been deliberate, since it happened just before he was killed.

"But wasn't his murder a professional hit?" he asked.

"Yes, but it wasn't over gambling debts."

"Then what was it over?"

"I don't know."

"What do you think it was over?"

"I don't know," she said with a sharper tone.

"No? No idea at all? Nothing?"

She pressed her mouth closed. Damn him. He was relentless. "The intruder broke in and caught my father unaware. There was no sign of forced entry. No prints. No witnesses. Nothing." Just like Kate.

"Why would anyone do that?"

She sighed her frustration. "Look, if I knew, I'd tell you, okay? I don't."

His amazing green eyes grew less menacing, her emotion reaching him. "Was he alone when he was killed?"

"Yes. My mother was out with her friends. Every week she went to dinner with them."

"What was he working on at the time?"

"I don't know."

"Don't you?" he asked gently.

If she told him the truth, he wouldn't believe her. She didn't know. Why would anyone want to kill her father? He didn't have a single enemy. He was a good man.

"Does Cullen know he was murdered?"

"Yes. Of course."

"Do you think his murder is related to Hersch?"

Oh, how she wished she could just tell him everything. How nice it would be if she had someone to lean on. Ever since Sage had died, she'd never leaned on anyone. She'd been in a fight for survival. Cullen had helped her, but she'd been in a shell. How had Jag seen that about her? He was the only one other than Cullen, maybe, who ever had. And it touched her in ways she couldn't organize in her mind. All she knew was that she was drawn to him.

As if sensing her turmoil, he turned her pivoting chair so that she faced him, using his knee on the outside of hers to keep her from swinging back toward the counter. "What are you so afraid of?"

Being wrong. But instead of telling him the way her instincts were clamoring for her to do, she just looked into his eyes. Maybe he'd seen the truth there.

"Have you ever trusted anyone?" he asked.

"Have you?"

"Yes, one time too many."

So they both had reason to guard their hearts. Odie found it oddly comforting. They had an understanding now. This didn't come easy but the bond between them had strengthened. She could lose herself in this moment. He leaned closer and pressed his lips to hers, a light and unexpected caress. But Odie wasn't resisting. She was too caught up in the moment. He pulled back and she met fire in his eyes before he kissed her again.

The room lost focus. The buzz of voices faded. All she felt was him kissing her.

The reminder of why she had to be guarded seeped through her passion. He was an operative who worked for Cullen. He was a soldier first. Love came second.

Pulling away, she stared up at him, frozen. Why had she allowed this to happen? Why had he? She could see the same confusion coming from him. She didn't welcome this sudden loss of control.

Pushing him, she freed enough room for her to swivel back toward the counter and then the other way. She jumped off the stool, walking as fast as she could to the door, ignoring stares on the way.

What was she thinking? How could she have let him kiss her like that? Did she want to fall for another man like Sage? No! It would kill her this time. She wouldn't survive another broken heart. As tough as everyone thought she was, she was as weak as a kitten when it came to love. Sometimes she wondered if she was even capable of loving anyone anymore. Not after the first time. The first time she'd loved without reservation. She'd held nothing back. The love she'd felt for her husband had been whole and consuming. And she'd welcomed it. Given everything she'd had to it. To him.

That had been a mistake. Loving a man who could be killed in an instant had been the worst mistake of her life. She would never put herself in that kind of situation again. Because she never wanted to feel what it was like to have that kind of love ripped out of her chest. Never again.

Odie's heart still hammered as she watched Jag stride toward the rental car where she waited for him. Looking up and down the street, he unlocked the doors with the fob he held. She'd already checked—the Lexus hadn't waited. She climbed into the car, lifting a laptop from the floor where Jag had put it. Jag didn't look at her as he started the car. His presence was like a generator, though, humming nearby, full of sexual energy.

She used the laptop for a diversion, activating the screen. "Huh," she grunted when she saw the GPS tracking software. "You don't waste any time."

"While you were in the restaurant with him, I put a magnetic transmitter on his truck."

Too bad they didn't have one for the Lexus. She saw

the indicator on the screen blinking. A street map with a blinking red dot showed Calan Friese's location. "He's on the move."

"Where is he?"

"Looks like he's heading out of town."

Jag started driving. The silence in the car was deafening.

"Odie…"

"Don't say it." He was going to apologize. She just knew it.

"How do you know what I'm going to say?" He sounded annoyed.

"You were going to talk about it. You know…*it*. And I don't want you to."

"I was just going to say you don't have to worry, it won't happen again."

"Good. Glad to hear it."

"Good." He sounded terse. "I'm glad you agree. The last thing I need is another go-round with someone who isn't who she's portrayed herself to be."

"Hey—what you see is what you get. I don't portray." Who had he gotten involved with that had portrayed herself falsely? Whoever she was, she must have made quite an impact for him to bring it up.

He sent her a dubious look. "Maybe not in your work, but your personal life…now that's a different story."

"I just don't want to get involved with someone who could get killed. What's so bad about that?"

He glanced derisively at her and faced forward again. "Let's just drop it. Stay focused on the job. Keep it professional. Can you do that?"

"Yes." But she wondered if that was true. Would her heart overrule that better judgment? Kissing him had made her feel something she hadn't felt since Sage. And that more than disconcerted her.

While her spirits fell, she looked down at the laptop screen and was glad to report a change. "Friese is heading toward Interstate 81."

"Looks like we're going on a road trip."

Great. Just what she needed, more time alone with him. She watched the laptop screen, but her mind kept wandering to that kiss. It had broken something loose, something she was good at keeping buried, until now.

Staring through the passenger window, she didn't really see the passing landscape. The last day she'd seen Sage descended upon her as if it had happened yesterday. He had stood in their foyer smiling as he held her.

"Two months isn't that long," he'd said.

"It will seem like forever." She'd looped her arms around his big shoulders, rising onto her toes to bring her mouth up to his. She'd been barefoot and wearing one of his button-down shirts and nothing else. They'd made love the night before and again that morning, but she could never get enough. And he was leaving.

"I don't want you to go," she'd told him, covering his face with kisses.

He'd put his hands on each side of her head. "I'll be back before you know it."

She'd shaken her head. "Don't go. Don't do it anymore. Find another job."

He'd chuckled. "You know this is what I do. There isn't anything else I want to do."

She'd kissed his mouth, wanting to convince him to stay.

"When I get home, I'll spend every second with you until

I have to leave again. Maybe we'll take a trip somewhere. The Caribbean or something."

She'd held on to that thought. Seeing him again. Two months. She could do it. Just two months….

Three weeks later they'd come knocking on the front door.

That was the one memory she wished she could forget. Usually she was pretty good at pushing it back where it belonged, in the dark shadows of her mind, far away from her conscience. But kissing Jag had brought it all back.

She'd opened the door and saw them in uniform. Two men. And she'd known.

"We're very sorry to tell you…"

She hadn't heard any more. She'd screamed and had kept screaming. Time had lost all order after that. Her mother had arrived. A doctor had given her a sedative. She'd spent two months at home. Well, most of the time that was where she'd been. She'd sat on the couch, ridden in her mother's car, sat outside. But she'd been in a daze. Numb. Dying inside. She'd nearly died from a broken heart. Her. Odelia Frank. Anyone who knew her now would never guess.

When she couldn't take it anymore, she'd convinced her mother that she was better and needed some time alone. But she was anything but better. She'd vanished in the Caribbean and would never have returned—lying listlessly in a secluded bungalow where no one was around. Death didn't scare her. It would relieve her of the pain.

As it turned out, her mother had told Cullen where she was, and he'd come to find her. He was looking for a good intelligence officer and had gotten her name from someone he knew, some government type who knew her father. He'd found her in the bungalow, skinny as a rail, uninterested in life.

"You okay?"

Odie flinched, her awareness returning to Jag. Feeling wetness on her cheek, she briskly wiped the tears, mortified that she'd allowed her thoughts to run away the way they had, and that they'd affected her like this.

"Fine."

Jag kept looking at her, glancing from the road to her.

"What the hell are you looking at?" she snapped.

"Why are you crying?"

"I'm not crying." Those few dribbles didn't count.

"I think I know when someone's crying."

"I wasn't crying. Crying is wailing and getting a stuffy nose. My eyes watered, that's all. Not that it's any of your damn business."

He glanced at her again but didn't say anything. He didn't have to. He was the first person since Cullen had found her crumbling under the weight of grief to see her one vulnerability. Sage and her love for him. And because of that, love in general.

Well, good. Great. Lovely. Now he knew why she couldn't get involved with him. She never wanted to feel like that again.

Chapter 5

Hours later, Jag drove the rental through the Monongahela National Forest near Harman, West Virginia. The tracker display showed Calan turning off the highway. It stopped moving a short distance up a dirt road.

Jag pulled to the side of the road at a long driveway leading up to a beautiful log home. Slipping on a pair of thin leather gloves, he pulled out a gun from his boot and opened the driver's door.

Odie opened the passenger door and followed him into the woods. The cabin came into view through a maze of tree trunks. The white truck was parked in the gravel drive in front of a garage.

Jag stopped. "Wait here."

"No. I'm going with you."

"You don't have a gun. I've been meaning to ask you why, too, by the way. Weren't you some kind of hotshot markswoman or something?"

Yes, but that was before Sage. "I don't need a gun." She started hiking again.

"No, you just need your mouth."

His teasing tone made her smile.

Moving ahead of her, Jag reached the sliding glass door in the back of the cabin. Odie heard the sound of a truck starting. Calan's? Was he leaving? Already?

She shared a glance with Jag.

He slid open the unlocked door and stepped inside. Odie searched the great room containing leather furniture and a huge fireplace. Tall windows offered a view of mountains from the back. There were no windows around the front door, but it was open a crack.

The cabin was quiet.

Odie's heart began to beat faster. This didn't feel right. The front door was open. Calan had just fled. And it was too quiet.

There were dishes piled in the kitchen sink and papers on the kitchen table. An empty bottle of beer sat on the coffee table before the fireplace. A throw blanket was crumpled on the couch. Someone was staying here.

She looked out the front window. Calan's white truck was gone. She moved to the garage door and opened it. There was a white Lexus inside. On the other side of the garage was a motorcycle.

"Jag?"

He came up behind her.

"Jesus," he muttered.

"Where is he?" If the man who'd come to Kate's funeral on that motorcycle—and followed them in that Lexus—was here, where was he now and why had Calan come to see him?

Jag turned and headed down a hallway across from the

living area, moving slowly and looking out the windows. She followed, instinctively knowing what they'd find. At the first door, he stopped. Odie peered inside. It was an office. The computer was on and the screensaver hadn't kicked in yet. On the floor a body of an older man lay facedown, blood staining the carpet around his head. Fresh blood. Whoever he was, he had just been killed. And it appeared as if Calan Friese had just done it.

"Damn it," Jag swore, going to the body. With his gloved hands, he rolled the man over.

Odie couldn't stop her sharp inhale. It was the man in the second picture she'd seen.

Jag glanced back at her and she tried to cover her alarm, but he was so astute when it came to observing her that she didn't doubt he'd picked up on something.

"You know him?"

She shook her head.

"Odie…"

"I swear I don't know him."

Anger tightened the line of his mouth. He glowered at her a moment longer and then began searching the body.

She turned to the computer, plucking a tissue from a box and putting it over the mouse. With a shaky hand, she maneuvered quickly, scanning files. Nothing unusual. On the desktop, she brought up the start menu and saw a link to a folder. Frasier Darby, it said. She went to the control panel and brought up the system window. Under computer name was Frasier Darby again.

"Anything?"

Realizing Jag stood behind her, she glanced back. "His name is Frasier Darby."

"I know, I have his driver's license."

Tucking the tissue into her pocket, she left the room

ahead of him. They searched the rest of the house. Odie let Jag do most the touching since he wore gloves. After about twenty minutes, nothing significant turned up.

"Come on. Let's go," Jag said, and she followed him through the front door, leaving it open a crack as it was when Friese had left. She jogged with Jag to their rental.

Inside, she put the laptop on her thighs and checked the monitor. "Friese went left."

"He's probably heading back to D.C.," Jag said.

"Let's not follow him. I want to be able to talk to him again."

"Don't you mean *we?*"

She sent him an impatient look while she used her satellite phone to call 911 and anonymously report the murder.

Just as she finished, the road led into a steeper grade. When Jag pressed the brakes, they didn't slow. He drove fast into a curve in the road.

"What's wrong?"

"Brakes aren't working."

Had someone punctured the line?

"Someone doesn't want to be followed," he said, shifting into Low.

The car slowed, but Jag had to steer hard to correct the direction of the car as it sailed out of the turn. The car swerved.

Odie saw the tree and shut her eyes as they hit it. Airbags exploded. She was disoriented for a second or two.

"You okay?" Jag asked as everything went still. The car engine sputtered and died.

"Yes."

Odie got out and stood under the branches of poplar trees. She looked over at Jag, who'd gotten out, too. She couldn't hear anything other than the sounds of wilderness carrying on as if they'd never come. She tipped her head back. There was a chill in the air and the sun was setting. She turned toward the road. It was desolate and full of deepening shadows. That didn't scare her. She knew self-defense and she was with one of TES's finest.

"I'll call Cullen. He can have someone arrange transportation, but it'll probably take them a while."

"I saw a turnoff to some cabins up the road," she offered.

"Works for me. Going to get dark soon." He bent into the rental and pulled out a duffel bag. She didn't have to see its contents to know it contained the essentials. His precaution didn't surprise her. Men like him were never caught unprepared.

She walked to the opposite rear door and opened it, grabbed her leather jacket and tote, seeing he'd also grabbed the laptop. Slinging the tote over one shoulder and draping the jacket over the other, she started walking up the road. Jag caught up to her in two or three easy strides.

"You think Friese killed that man?" she asked.

"Looks that way to me."

"Yeah, but I didn't hear a gunshot."

"He could have used a silencer."

"And then punctured our brake line?" Unless someone else had gotten there ahead of Friese, that's what had likely happened.

"We'll go with that for now."

She nodded. "But let's not discount other possibilities. Friese would have had to have killed that man really fast."

"Gone in and pulled the trigger. Yep."

It hadn't looked as if the man had struggled. Shot in the back of the head.

She looked to her side at the darkening forest, where rhododendron and mountain laurel spread beneath the canopy, and then ahead at the dirt road that curved into the trees and disappeared. Her father had been killed on a road like that.

Now that the excitement of the afternoon had passed, and all he had to occupy his mind was a long walk in the dark with Odie, Jag couldn't stop his thoughts from wandering back to that kiss. He still couldn't figure out what had made him do it. It hadn't even mattered that they were in a busy restaurant, either. She refused to tell him everything she knew about her father's murder and that made her seem shady. He didn't think she was keeping anything from him about Friese, but if she did learn something he doubted she'd share it without him prying it out of her.

Though he couldn't deny his growing attraction to her, he had to consider the worst. If what she was hiding was related to Hersch, it wouldn't paint her in very favorable light. Had her father been involved in something unscrupulous before he was killed? Or had he discovered something bigger than he could handle? The way Odie was behaving, he'd go with the former. But would she hinder a TES investigation for personal reasons? He had a hard time imagining her willing to do such a thing. But then, it might be her father's reputation on the line. How far would she go to protect it?

He checked Odie to see how she was holding up. They'd walked about ten miles so far. She didn't seem bothered. And then he felt silly for thinking she couldn't keep up with him. He had to admit, that part about her appealed to him. He'd never met anyone like her. She was tough and capable, and then there was a softer side he doubted very few people ever saw.

"Are you going to tell me why you don't carry a gun?" he asked. It was a good way to lead into other questions he had for her.

"No."

"Why not?"

"I don't want to."

She was like a guy that way. Brief and to the point. Very little emotion. Always logical and on the mark. Not that every guy was like that, but those who worked for TES were. "Do you have any guns at your house?"

"No."

"Keep any at TES headquarters?"

"Nope."

He turned to see her. She kept her profile to him and her face void of reaction. "Is it because your husband was killed in action?"

Abruptly, she stopped. He was slower to do the same. Bingo.

"How do you do that?" she asked.

"Do what?"

"Guess everything."

He shrugged. "Common sense."

"It's annoying."

He smiled, unable to help it. Other than the loss of her husband, she said whatever was on her mind and didn't waste much time tiptoeing around feelings. He didn't realize how much he liked that in a woman until now. If only that extended to the connection between Hersch and her father.

She started walking again and he fell in step beside her.

"How long ago did he die?"

"Your common sense is faltering."

He did his own math. "You've been with TES what... almost six years now?"

She stopped walking again, this time folding her arms, her dark eyes beaming with challenge.

So, her husband had died about six years ago. "That's a long time."

Her brow lifted. He ignored it. She needed to be pushed every once in a while.

"Was that engineer the first man you've been with since then?"

"And this is your business...how?"

"I'm just curious. You don't have to answer."

"I've dated other men over the last couple of years."

So for four of those years she hadn't been interested in anyone. "But no operatives."

"I dated a couple of those, too. At first."

Was that why she'd cried in the car earlier? Had she been thinking of her husband? What had made her think of him? Being with an operative again? Kissing one and liking it?

Had she felt it that much? He sure as hell had.

He caught himself. "You're right. It's none of my business." He started walking again. He didn't want to desire a woman who kept secrets, especially one with Odelia Frank's background. She could be dangerous. Why did it matter what she thought of him? It didn't. At least, it shouldn't.

She caught up to him, her long, dark hair shiny and thick and swinging with her movement. She didn't wear makeup but her dark eyes were striking on her smooth, proportioned face. She'd put on her leather jacket. One hand swung free at her side and she had her work tote hanging from her other shoulder. She had great thighs, long and toned in those faded jeans. She always wore hiking boots, too. He'd like to see her in high heels.

Catching himself again, he looked ahead.

It was a still night. No clouds. The stars were far away, not as bright as they were in Roaring Creek. The elevation here was so much lower.

"Don't take it personally," she said.

What did she think he was thinking? "Take what personally?"

"I just don't like talking about him, that's all."

"That's okay, I don't like talking about my ex-wife, either."

"You were married?"

He saw her surprise. "Do you think every man in my profession isn't marriage material?"

"No. Not if they work for TES. There must be something in the water in Roaring Creek."

"So, there *is* hope for you."

"I drink bottled water."

He chuckled. Damn, he liked her mind. He walked without saying anything for a while, but he could tell she wanted to know more.

"When did you get divorced?" she asked.

"Three years ago." He really didn't want to talk about this. Maybe he should have avoided the topic of her husband.

"What happened? She get tired of you always being gone?"

"No." But he'd bet that's what she hadn't liked about her marriage.

"What then? Is she the one who portrayed herself as someone she wasn't?"

He contemplated not answering. Out of fairness, he did. "She was arrested for a hit-and-run."

Odie whistled and looked at him with incredulous eyes. "She ran from an accident?"

"One that killed a woman and her son. She went to prison for it."

"Oh, my God, that's terrible."

"She was also into drugs. I didn't know any of that until after I married her. I didn't know about the accident or her drug dealings. Not until the cops came knocking one day."

"Didn't you spend enough time to get to know her?"

"She told me she was an English teacher who'd just moved to the East Coast and was looking for a job. She said her parents were killed in a car wreck and she didn't have any siblings. The truth was her mother was a hooker who couldn't identify daddy without a DNA test. She grew up in a poor suburb of Detroit. Her first husband abused her and was unfaithful. That's when she got into drugs. I didn't even know she'd been married before. She was running from the law when I met her. But of course, she didn't tell me that."

"How long were you married?"

"Six months."

"I won't ask anything stupid, like, did you love her."

Figures, she'd have to say something smart. "Thanks."

She smiled.

And it lifted his mood.

Spotting a sign ahead, he pointed. "There are the cabins."

* * *

Odie stepped up the stairs onto the front porch of the cabin they'd rented. There were two left and Jag had paid for the one with two bedrooms. If he'd have picked the one-bedroom cabin, she'd have said something. There was no restaurant here, but plenty of fish. The woman who'd checked them in had given her the fish her husband had caught that morning. She'd also succumbed to Jag's charm and handed over a pasta salad and a bottle of wine.

Inside the cabin, Odie turned on a light. A small living room with a gas fireplace in the corner was sparsely furnished with a brown sofa and chair with a lamp next to it. One picture hung on the wall. Stairs near the door led to a loft, off which were two bedrooms.

Odie went through the living room to the kitchen and searched for a pan to cook the fish in. She turned on the oven and a few minutes later put the fish inside. The sound of a cork being freed from a bottle made her turn and smile.

Jag poured wine into two glasses and handed her one.

"Who'd have thought we'd be vacationing tonight?" She sipped the wine, a good Chardonnay.

She eyed Jag's chest and biceps in the black henley.

"Yeah, all alone with a woman who can shoot better than me and probably give me a black eye." He looked down at her boots. "Sexy shoes, too."

"You like them," she said. "Admit it."

"You prefer your women more flowery?"

He didn't agree or disagree, but she could tell he did like her shoes. It made her wonder what kind of woman he was attracted to.

"What was your wife like? Do you mind me asking?"

"You're asking if I mind?"

She leaned her butt against the stove. "What was she like?"

He grinned. "Actually, she was a lot like you." He moved to stand in front of her. "Not that I'm comparing you to a criminal. I just mean she was outdoorsy and independent. Strong-willed. Tough."

So, he liked women like that? Women like her? "I pictured you with someone more feminine than that. You know, the kind that can't kill spiders."

His grin renewed and he nodded as if to some kind of irony he'd found in that. "I've found that most women like that are too afraid of me."

"I don't always dress like this." She looked down at her jeans and boots.

"Did you wear a dress for the nerd?"

"No. He never took me anywhere fancy."

"He probably didn't think you'd want to."

That was probably true. "Do you think you'll ever get married again?" His last marriage might have tainted him.

"Sure. If the right woman comes along. I'm going to be a lot more careful next time, though."

"Who can blame you?" He probably felt as if he had to be careful with her.

"What got you into this kind of work, anyway?" she asked, changing the subject.

He lowered the glass after taking a sip. "When I was growing up I was interested in everything going on in the world. I read the paper, watched news programs, and read all kinds of books. I wanted to get into politics and maybe work my way to Congress, but I was too restless for that. I also wanted to travel the world and try new things. That's why I joined the navy."

"What about the world intrigues you?"

"*Intrigue* might not be the best word. *Pissed off* does a better job."

"What kinds of things pissed you off?"

"You already know. Terrorism, poverty, dictatorship. Reading about those kinds of things made me feel lucky to be an American. It's a little clichéd, but I wanted to fight to preserve what made this country what it is."

He believed in the foundation of America and wanted to fight for it. Make a difference. Why did that appeal to her so much? It never appealed to her in other men like him, so why was he so different? She'd never noticed it in other men. She'd never really spent any time with men like him, either. Sure, she'd dated, but that had never lasted and she'd never allowed the conversations to go very far. Since Sage died, she'd been so sensitive to men like him. Guarded.

"Did you ever wish you'd have chosen another career?" she asked.

He shook his head. "I've never regretted it. But I'm not going to do this type of work much longer."

That got her attention. "Why not?"

"I'm getting older for one thing. There are other things that interest me, for another."

"What things?"

"You're awfully curious for someone who can't stand guys like me."

Yes, but he wasn't like the others she'd met. The more she got to know him, the more that was true. And now he was telling her he wasn't planning to work for TES much longer. For a moment she actually considered the possibility of pursuing him. Then a familiar sensation circled and plunged in her stomach, something dark, a reminder of how she'd felt in those months after Sage died.

For the first time since then, love seemed possible again. Really and truly love. Not like it was with the nerd. That wasn't love. She'd almost married that engineer because she'd felt safe with him. There was never the threat of loving him the way she'd loved Sage. But Jag…

"I like to cook and fix old motorcycles," he said.

"You cook?"

"My dad owned a bakery. I learned at a young age how to make great bread. Some day I'd like to open one."

"Huh." She took in his big frame and rugged face, marveling. "I'd have never guessed."

"I fix up old bikes, too." He sounded worried about what she thought.

"That saves your masculinity."

He grunted a laugh. "I like to woodwork, too. I've built furniture."

"Wow. The tourists would love you in Roaring Creek. Fresh bread, furniture. And motorcycles, too."

"I thought you hated that town."

"I struggle between love and hate."

"You do strike me as more of a big-city girl." His eyes went on an unhurried journey down her body, lingering on her boots before returning to her face.

She smiled. "I do miss D.C."

"Do you regret going to work for Cullen?"

She shook her head. "No."

"Did you want to leave the army?"

She knew what he was asking. Did she want to leave after her husband died or had she simply been unable to do her job? "I've never regretted going to work for Cullen. The only regret I have is that he relocated to a remote mountain town."

Sipping her wine, she watched him read between the

lines of her answer. No, she hadn't wanted to leave, but she was happy where it had taken her. She let the conversation go quiet for a while. He moved to a window and peered outside, sipping his wine. She watched him until she realized more than a half hour had passed.

She faced the stove and removed the cooked fish, while he got some plates and put the unfinished bottle of wine on the table.

They sat and ate in silence. Odie stole a few looks at him. She was uncomfortable over how easy it was being with him all of a sudden.

"Don't get any ideas, okay?" she said.

He stopped chewing to look at her. "About what?"

"You and me."

Leaning back, he finished what was left in his glass. Then he lifted the bottle and poured more into her glass first before filling his.

"Why would I get ideas, Odie? You're always reminding me how lacking I am as a TES operative."

Yes, but he'd just told her he wasn't going to do that much longer. "We're getting along."

"Would you rather fight?"

"You know what I mean. This is starting to feel…I don't know…off."

He breathed a laugh, sounding cynical, and shook his head as he ate more fish.

"Don't you think it seems different?" she pressed.

"What's the matter, afraid you're going to start liking me?"

"I'm not afraid. You're the one who should be afraid. I'm just trying to save you some grief."

"I appreciate your thoughtfulness, but I think I can watch out for myself."

"I'm not having sex with you."

"We might not be able to control ourselves." He was still joking.

"I'll be able to control myself. Stop trying to be funny."

"I wasn't. You're overreacting."

"I'm overreacting."

"Yeah. I don't want to have sex with you, either."

And she immediately knew why. He had been married to a woman who hid things from him. He obviously wouldn't want to make the same mistake twice.

"Right. It's a silly concern." She leaned back in her chair and drank some more wine, disconcerted by her sense of disappointment.

"When are you going to tell me how you know Frasier Darby?"

Back to business. Odie took her plate and put it in the sink. That was her answer. She wasn't going to tell him.

Chapter 6

Odie stirred when she heard a sound outside her window. It took her a moment to remember where she was. She lifted her head and listened. Something clattered. Pulling the covers off her too-warm body she swung her feet onto the cold wood floor. After looking out the window and seeing nothing, she went to the door. Jag's room door was open. Moving to the loft railing, she saw him peering through the narrowly open front door. His gun was drawn.

She watched him open the door wider and step out onto the front porch. Was someone out there? Her muscles tensed and her heart picked up a few extra beats. Feeling the chilled mountain air drift over her skin, she pulled her button-down stretch shirt tighter and went down the stairs.

Outside, she shivered and stayed close to the door. Jag appeared from around the corner of the cabin, gun lowered.

His head moved as he searched the night. He wore only a pair of jeans.

That's when she remembered she was only wearing a shirt and underwear. Seeing her, his steps slowed as his eyes took her in, lingering on her long legs and bare feet. A warm response flared in her.

"What are you doing out here?" she asked.

He took the steps slowly and stopped a couple of feet from her. "I heard a noise."

"I heard something, too."

"It was the people in the cabin next to ours. Two young couples, and they're drinking. One of them went to the office for firewood. They keep bundles outside for guests. I think they're having a bonfire."

It was a nice night for a fire, cool for late summer. "You heard them getting wood?"

"I heard them when they passed our cabin."

He must have really good ears, or his training had kicked in. Sleeping on the edge of alertness probably came secondhand to him. Special ops man that he was...

The reminder did little to stave her awareness of him. She glanced down at his bare chest and the perfect fit of his jeans at the waist. It was as if she were becoming desensitized to her aversion to his type. Either that, or it didn't matter so much anymore.

Raising her eyes, she caught his moving up from checking out her lower regions. The energy heated up between them.

She pointed to the still open door. "We should..."

"Yeah."

Going inside, she stopped at the base of the stairs while

he closed the door. They just stared at each other, gazes locked. Odie resisted the urge to look her fill over his entire body. His quiet patience was equally tantalizing, intelligence and brawn blending to make an intriguing package. He observed her expertly. Read her. No man had ever learned her as quickly as he had. She watched him look down her body and meet her eyes again. She met those captivating green orbs and was afraid her passion showed.

He took a step forward and her heart fluttered anew. She stepped backward up the first stair. He stopped at the bottom of them. Turning, she climbed up to the loft, but paused there to look down at him. Still holding his gun, he put his other hand on the railing and trailed it along the wood as he climbed up after her. At the top, he stood close.

She couldn't move. The desire in his eyes mirrored her own. All she had to do was take his hand and lead him into her room. She wanted that with such urgency she almost forgot why it was a bad idea.

They'd both declared they didn't want to sleep together, and yet here they were, on the verge of doing just that.

"Jag…"

"Good night, Odie." Walking past her, he went into his room and shut the door.

Going to her room, she shut the door behind her. Breathing deep breaths, she turned and leaned her back against the door, closing her eyes and fighting what felt both right and wrong at the same time. Confusion. She had to get her head straight regarding Jag. Was she ready to give another operative a try? Nothing much frightened her, but that did.

* * *

The rain was incessant. Outside the internet café, the sky was dark and everything was dripping wet. Odie tapped away on her laptop keyboard, occasionally checking around her to make sure no one noticed she was pretending to be busy. This morning she'd text messaged a computer savvy friend who worked at the IRS. Finally she'd convinced her to send over what she needed.

She and Jag had gotten back from their cabin stay late yesterday. This morning she'd waited for him to get in the shower before she dug in his duffel bag for Frasier Darby's driver's license. After writing all the information down and replacing the wallet in the bag, she'd managed to sneak away.

She'd given her contact at the IRS Frasier's name and the address on his driver's license a while ago. Now she was getting impatient. She checked her watch. Almost ten.

Her cell phone beeped the tone that let her know a text message had come through. She opened it.

Check your email.

Odie entered her internet email account and saw a message from her contact.

Yes! she wanted to shout out loud. She picked up her phone and replied to her friend.

The usual thank-you is on its way.

It was their unspoken agreement. Bribery did work. Especially for a woman with three kids, no husband and a low-paying job. Five hundred would go a long way.

Odie opened the email.

Frasier Darby. Two addresses. One matched the location of the cabin. He was an engineer. Retired at fifty-six. Must have managed his money well. Married. No kids. Odie frowned. What did he have to do with Kate?

Her contact gave her the name of his wife. She didn't work, either. She hadn't been at the cabin. Trouble in paradise? Odie did an internet search of the D.C. address. It wasn't far from here. An apartment in Georgetown.

"So you didn't know who he was."

Odie jumped, still seated on the chair, and whipped her head around. Jag stood there, reading the printout of the email. He'd picked it up from the printer.

"How the hell…?" She just couldn't shake him.

His eyes rose to look at her over the printout. "I know you."

"There are how many internet cafés in D.C.?"

"I knew you'd go to one of three. This is the second one I've been to."

She should have known he'd find her. And damn if she didn't like that. She tried not to gobble him up with her eyes, but it was impossible. He looked good in dark blue jeans and a white T-shirt, and his eyes were glowing with responding awareness.

"Who is he?" he asked, and there was a flirtatious lilt in his tone.

The night at the cabin had sure turned up the heat a notch. She couldn't be near him and not feel the sizzle. "Nobody from what I can tell." She looked at his hand holding the email. He kept his fingernails clean and trimmed.

"An engineer."

"Yeah." She loved his green eyes. "It doesn't make sense."

"You want to go talk to his wife?"

"You're incorrigible, you know that?" But secretly she was thrilled he was going with her.

He grinned. "Come on. I have the rental out front."

* * *

By early afternoon, Odie walked with Jag toward the entrance of a redbrick and white trim apartment building in Georgetown. Heather Darby lived on the fifth floor. All the way here she kept telling herself to stop drooling over Jag.

His long strides weren't that much longer than hers, because she was pretty tall. She liked the way he moved. For as muscular as he was, he was agile. He knew how to handle her, too. He had a way of talking to her, and staying close even when she tried to get away. He calmed her. Made her forget her pact to never involve herself with an operative again.

There she went again. Drooling.

Stop, she told herself.

After riding the elevator with four other people, they approached Heather's apartment. The front door opened and two men exited, one carrying camera gear. A reporter had come with a cameraman to talk to Heather about Frasier Darby's death.

Odie watched the reporter. He looked familiar. As he passed, he seemed to recognize her, too. That's when it hit her.

He smiled and stopped, about to strike up a conversation, but Odie kept walking. She didn't like reporters. Not after Cullen's identity had been exposed after rescuing his wife from Afghanistan. It had nearly caused TES to crumble, but Cullen had renamed and restructured his business and saved it. That reporter had been the one to catch him declaring his everlasting love to Sabine, who was now his wife and the mother of his cute little girl.

"They didn't waste any time," Jag commented as they stopped at the door.

A fiftyish woman with dyed brown hair stood in the still open doorway. Her eyes were red from crying.

"Heather Darby?" Odie asked.

"No." The woman glanced behind her, where two women sat on a living-room sofa. One wiped her eyes and sniffed as she looked toward the door, and the other had her hand on the sobbing woman's back. That must be Heather.

A wiry man stood on the other side of the coffee table, hands stuffed into his jeans pockets.

"I'm Odelia Frank and this is Jag Benney," Odie said to the woman at the door, but loud enough for all to hear. She didn't think there was any danger in revealing their real names. Besides, that reporter had recognized her. There was no point in lying. "We'd like to talk to Heather about her husband."

The brown-haired woman glanced back at the crying woman again and then shook her head. "It's really not a good time."

"Please. We just need to ask her a few questions."

"Frasier was murdered yesterday. We just got back from the coroner's and identified the body. Reporters just left…"

"Yes, we know, and we're very sorry, ma'am, but it's important we talk to Heather. We may be able to help."

"How do you know Frasier?"

"He came to us for help before he was killed."

Jag looked at her when she spoke the lie.

"Help for what?"

"Please, can we talk to Heather?"

The woman hesitated. "Just a minute." She left the door open and went to crouch before the dark-haired woman crying on the sofa.

"It's okay," the tearful woman said. She was almost

identical in appearance to the one who'd answered the door. Twins. Not identical, fraternal, but uncannily similar in appearance. Wiping her eyes with her hand, she stood and approached the door, taking a tissue from the wiry man on the way and dabbing her nose with it.

"Why did Frasier come to you for help?" she asked.

"Can you tell us why he was at the cabin?" Odie countered, ignoring the question.

Large, bulbous tears bloomed in her eyes and spilled over onto her face. Her breath hitched in a pathetic whimper.

"I…I kicked him out of the apartment," she wailed.

Her twin sister rushed to her side and put her arm around her shoulders. Then to them she said, "Maybe you should come back tomorrow. She's had enough for one day."

"No." Heather shrugged free of her twin's embrace. "It's okay. If they can help, I want to talk to them." To Jag and Odie, she asked, "Have you spoken with the police? They were here last night."

"Not yet. We wanted to talk to you first." It was a lie, of course. The police would only slow everything down. "Why did you kick him out?"

"I asked him for a divorce. He was having an affair. He was always coming home late and then one night he just didn't come home at all. He confessed to me the next day." She dabbed more tears with the tissue.

"I'm sorry to hear that," Odie said.

The woman looked from her to Jag. "Why did Frasier go to you for help?"

"I'm afraid we can't divulge that."

"Why not? It might have something to do with his murder."

"Yes, it very well could, and we'll do all we can to

find his killer, but we can't discuss certain aspects of our investigation."

"What kind of investigation? Are you detectives?"

"Who was he having an affair with?" Jag asked, effectively ending the question.

Heather looked at Jag. "I don't know her. I don't want to know her. He's a son of a bitch for cheating on me. When I first found out, I wished he was dead." She burst into a wave of fresh tears and her sister put her arm around her again. "I wanted him to be miserable."

Couldn't get any more miserable than dead. "Did you ever see her?" Odie asked.

"No."

"Did you ever notice anything odd about Frasier's behavior? Other than his affair, I mean."

"No. He was good at keeping his other life a secret."

"His other life, meaning his affair?"

"Yes." Odie thought any woman who ignored signs like her husband coming home late all the time and never calling her didn't want to face the truth. And Heather hadn't. Not until the truth had forced her. Her husband had confessed.

"Did you or Frasier ever know a man named Calan Friese?" she asked.

Heather thought a moment. Then she shook her head. "No. I've never heard that name before. Who is he?"

"Someone we think your husband might have known," Odie answered neutrally.

"How would he have known him?" She looked from Odie to Jag. "Why did he go to you for help? You have to tell me. We may have been having problems, but I loved him." She gasped for air as she began crying again. "I still love him." Her crying became uncontrollable.

Her sister looked imploringly at Odie.

"We'll come back later."

The woman nodded. "Thank you."

When the door closed, Odie left the apartment building ahead of Jag. Outside, she noticed a white truck parked on the other side of a flower bed with a tree in the middle. No one was inside.

"Look."

He followed her nod. "What's he doing here?"

"Why would he want to talk to Heather?" Odie asked.

"Maybe because we did."

"Did he see us go into the building?"

"Must have."

"You'd think he'd stay far away after killing Heather's husband."

"Yeah, you'd think. If he was the one who killed Frasier."

Good point. What if Calan hadn't killed Frasier? He could have walked in on a murder the same way she and Jag had.

Jag remained parked where he was. "Let's give him a few minutes."

Good idea. After about forty minutes, Calan emerged from the building, glancing their way before climbing into his truck.

"Well, he obviously doesn't care that we saw him."

"He knows we'll go back up and talk to Heather."

"And he isn't worried. Huh." She got out of the rental with Jag.

They walked back into the apartment building. Up the elevator and down the hall, Jag knocked.

Heather opened the door, more composed than the first time. "You're back."

"Calan Friese was just here," Odie said. "What did he want?"

She looked warily from Odie to Jag. "He asked why the two of you were just here."

"Did you tell him?"

Heather's sister appeared beside her like the first time.

"I told him Frasier went to you for help and you wanted to know why he went to the cabin," Heather said.

"Did you tell him your husband was having an affair?"

"He said Frasier didn't go to you two for help," she said with a hint of accusation.

"Did you tell him your husband was having an affair?" Odie repeated. She didn't want Calan to know they'd be looking for the woman. If he killed Frasier, he might kill her, too, to keep her from talking.

"He also said Odelia Frank had her own agenda and it didn't include Frasier's welfare." Then she turned to Jag. "He said she probably had you fooled."

Jag glanced at Odie and she could see his chagrin.

"Who are you?" Heather asked. "How did you know Frasier? Why did he go to you for help?"

"I'm afraid we can't divulge that. We're from a private organization, but we *are* investigating your husband's murder. I'm guessing Mr. Friese isn't comfortable with that and that's why he came to see you."

She contemplated them. It wasn't much, but it was a vague explanation. Maybe it would be enough.

She exchanged a look with her sister and then turned to them. "He said Frasier was involved in something over his head and it got him killed."

"That much is true."

"What was it?"

"Did he ask you anything else?" Odie asked instead of answering. "Is there anything else you told him that you haven't told us?"

Heather looked from Jag to Odie and then shook her head. "No."

"Thank you very much, Heather. You've been a big help. And again, we're very sorry for your loss." Odie started to turn, looking at Jag and telling him with her eyes that she thought Heather wasn't saying something.

He returned it with a similar look.

"What was Frasier doing that got him killed?"

Odie pivoted and faced Heather again. She didn't answer. Telling her too much would only put her in danger.

"Right," Heather said derisively. "You can't divulge that."

"I'm sorry," Odie said.

"Are you government? Calan Friese didn't seem like he was, but you two do. He sort of scared me. There was something about him, you know?" She made a distasteful face.

"Again, thank you for your time, Heather." Odie turned with Jag and they started down the walkway. There wasn't anything else to say, and Heather didn't trust them.

"Wait a minute."

Excitement and hope soared inside Odie. She knew when someone was about to spill something.

"I lied to Mr. Friese. Frasier did go see a man once. A colonel in the army. Roth, I think was his name."

Chills prickled up and down Odie's arms. She knew Colonel Roth.

"I thought it was strange," Heather went on. "I mean, why was he going to see an officer in the military?"

"When did Frasier go talk to the colonel?"

"I don't know." Heather paused as she thought. "Maybe a month ago. I kicked him out of the house shortly after that."

"Thank you. You don't know what a big help you've been today. We'll be in touch."

She and Jag left the building.

"Oh, my God." Odie had trouble catching her breath after she and Jag got into the car.

"What's the matter?" Instead of driving away, he kept the rental in park and looked over at her.

"Colonel *Roth?*"

"What about him?"

Jag recognized the name but didn't understand the degree of her reaction. Of course he didn't. Colonel Roth ran a Special Projects Directorate for Army Special Operations Command, but only she and Cullen knew how he was connected to TES. It was huge. Why was an engineer who was having an affair with a mysterious woman want to seek out someone like that?

"Let's go talk to him," Jag said.

She'd love to, but no way. "He'll never agree to see us."

Jag sent her a sharp look. "Why not?"

She just shook her head, overwhelmed with the implications. Roth had asked Cullen to look into Hersch *after* he'd met with Frasier. Had the colonel known there was a connection? Maybe not. Without being able to talk to Frasier, she might never find out.

"Odie…?"

Jag thought she was deliberately withholding information again. "Hey, if you want to know anything about Roth, you're going to have to ask Cullen. I'm not saying a word unless he approves."

"Cullen?"

"Yes."

"Okay, let's call him then." When Odie didn't move, he said, "Go on, call him right now."

If she didn't call him, he'd only be more convinced that she was hiding a dark side. He didn't trust her and that would make it worse. But if she did call Cullen, what then? She'd risk him asking too many questions. She didn't have to answer, not yet, and Cullen already suspected something since she ran off to D.C. without Jag, defying his orders. So, really she had nothing to lose. And Cullen might tell her something important about Roth.

She found her cell and called. Her hands trembled. Her nerves felt like live wires whipping and lashing in her body. It made her nauseous. All the while Jag noticed. And he thought it was attributed to her secrets.

"Odie. You have something to report?" Cullen asked as soon as he answered.

Her heart slammed behind her rib cage. "Who asked you to look into Hersch, Cullen?" she asked, even though she already knew.

"Excuse me? You know we never discuss that. What are you doing, Odie? You went to D.C. on your own and now you're digging where you don't belong. You're beginning to test my patience."

"Jag and I just left Heather Darby's house." Odie knew she had to talk fast. "Frasier Darby was her husband. We followed Calan to his cabin and found him dead."

"Who the hell is Frasier Darby?"

So, he didn't know. Odie was relieved, and then she felt guilty because she was withholding information from him and he was not. He'd taken his orders from Roth and passed them on to her and Jag.

"He was an engineer who was having an affair with someone we have yet to identify. Heather said that's the reason she kicked him out. He cheated on her."

"That's all fine for daytime television, Odie. Why did you call me?"

"Heather said Frasier went to talk to Colonel Roth about a month ago."

Silence stretched over the line.

"Whatever you do, don't go anywhere near him, Odie," he finally said.

"We have to talk to him."

"No, we don't. He had a reason for putting us on to Hersch. Do your job and leave him out of it. Do you understand what I'm saying?"

"Yes."

"You do what I tell you and stay away from Roth."

"Cullen—"

"Something like this could ruin TES. You of all people should know that."

"Yes, I do know. But look at what we have so far. Kate was murdered. Her boyfriend may have killed some Joe Blow engineer who went to see Roth a month ago. But Roth never mentioned it when he asked you to look into Hersch. He's connected, Cullen. He knows more than he told you."

Another long silence ensued. "If you're suggesting he might be dirty…"

"No, I'm not. But he *is* protecting *something* or *someone*, and I think the woman Darby was having an affair with is the key."

"Why her?"

"Because it fits. Darby doesn't run in the same circles as Kate, but whoever he was sleeping with must."

"You don't know who she is."

"No." Her heart sank because she knew what he was going to say next.

"Then that's where you need to focus your energy. I mean it, Odie. You could crucify this organization if you aren't careful."

"I know that. Don't you think I know that? After all the publicity your wife's rescue mission generated? That almost killed us then."

"This is personal to you."

"It was personal for you, too."

"Damn it, Odie, don't pull your crap on me right now."

She bit back a retort. Why was he keeping her away from Roth?

"Tell me why you went to D.C. without Jag," Cullen said. "Then maybe I'll listen to ideas of talking to Roth."

Odie closed her eyes. Maybe it was time. He'd always been her rock. The one who never let her down, and trusted her implicitly. He waited for her to tell him now. But she couldn't. She was too afraid.

"What do you want me to tell Jag?" she asked instead.

"Don't tell him who Roth is. I regret ever telling you."

That stung. But he disconnected before she could say more.

She lowered her phone and stared down at it in her hand. How was she going to avoid telling Jag? The strange thing was...she wanted to tell him.

"Well?" he said.

"He doesn't want me to tell you."

Jag sighed hard. "That figures. I should be getting used to this by now."

She looked over at him. "Roth is connected to TES."

He stared at her. "What?"

Odie's heart hammered hard and fast. "He's the one who asked Cullen to look into Hersch."

Jag just stared at her.

"That's way more than I should have told you. If Cullen found out, he'd ruin me. He goes to great pains to keep the identities of his contacts in the government secret. It's imperative to the survival of TES."

"I won't say a word, Odie. And if you can tell me that, why can't you tell me about your father?"

In that instant, she knew she could. "Because I'm afraid he's linked to Hersch somehow. I know something that could prove he was involved with someone really terrible, but I'm almost ninety-nine percent sure he was set up."

"Almost?" He sounded angry. "Who might he have been involved with?"

It scared her to even say the name. "Abu Dharr al-Majid. He heads a Zaidi rebel group believed to be funded by the Iranians." She hesitated. "I've done some digging and it looks like…it looks like…" She couldn't finish.

"It looks like what, Odie?" Jag demanded.

She looked over at him. "I recently found ties to… other…more well-known terrorists."

Jag's mouth tightened and she could tell he fought his temper. "And you kept that from TES?"

"Dharr was on our Watch List."

"But ties to terrorism removes them from the Watch. He belongs in Surveillance now. You hindered that progress by keeping it a secret. Dharr could have been stopped long before now."

He was furious.

"I would have turned him in to Surveillance. But I got that package. I just wanted to check some things out first."

That wasn't enough to placate him. He still looked at her with disgust and anger.

"Jag, please try to understand what I was dealing with. My father wouldn't have gotten involved with someone like that."

"Your father is dead."

"Yes, and even in death someone out there wants him to be their scapegoat. I want to uncover the truth, but I don't want his reputation tarnished."

"What makes you think he met with Dharr?"

"Kate found pictures of him meeting him in Yemen. An anonymous source sent them to her after she did some fishing."

"So someone wanted you to find out."

"Yes. And that's what convinced me it was a setup. My father looks like the bad guy, when in fact he's not."

"Or so you hope." His disgust with her hurt more than she expected. "How long have you known this?"

"Kate found someone in Yemen last year. That someone went to the anonymous source and that's when we received the photos. But there's more." She hesitated. This wasn't going to go over well. Jag looked over at her and cocked his head in disbelief. "After my father was killed, I found an email he'd sent." She didn't want to finish.

"What did the email say?"

"It said, 'Meet me at my house. We'll discuss logistics there.' A time was specified and it matches when he was killed."

"So, you think someone other than your father sent it from his computer."

"Yes." Dharr. "I was able to trace it to Yemen, but I never located the source. I think Dharr sent it and then killed him."

"What did you do with the email?"

She pressed her lips closed and looked out the window.

"You got rid of it?" He sounded incredulous.

"I have all I need up here." She tapped her head with her forefinger.

"What about the pictures?"

She looked out the windshield this time.

"You got rid of them?" he shouted. And then swore.

"I was conducting my own investigation. The police were going nowhere. It would have been a waste of time to rely on them. I wanted to find my father's killer and that email and those photos were a setup."

Jag didn't ask any more questions. He was too steaming mad. She all but felt it radiating off him.

"You should have come clean from the start, Odie."

"Don't you think I know that?" she yelled. "How do you think I felt when Kate sent me that file on Hersch?"

"So you did see it."

"No. I told you the truth. I didn't see everything, I saw the picture of Hersch and another of a man I didn't recognize. Frasier Darby. I withheld that because I wanted to know who he was first."

"How did you know Hersch was connected to your dad?"

"I didn't. Not exactly. Kate wrote some initials on the package. It was our code. She wrote ELF on the return address whenever something was related to my father."

"And you didn't get a chance to find out how."

"No."

Again, Jag didn't say anything for a while. "All right. I can see why you were so worried. And maybe even why you felt like you had to keep it from me."

"From everyone."

"But you shouldn't have kept something like Dharr a secret. It could be the missing piece."

He meant about her father's murder. That touched a deep and warm place in her heart. Instead of focusing only on the things she'd withheld, he was more concerned with helping her find her father's killer. Or did he think her father's killer could also be Kate's? And the key to taking down Hersch.

Had she been so wrapped up in protecting her father's innocence that she'd missed that? "What do you think we should do?"

"What we were supposed to do from the beginning. Get inside Hersch's organization and see what turns up."

"You can't work for him. He might be the one who sent that man after the package Kate sent me."

"We'll keep out of sight. Watch him for a while. Tap into his communications. Take a look inside Defense Initiatives."

They would have gotten to that point eventually anyway. Kate's murder had only delayed things.

They reached the hotel and got into the elevator. They were alone.

"What would you have done if you discovered your father was really doing business with Dharr?" Jag asked, pressing the button for their floor.

"I would have told Cullen."

He looked doubtful.

She met his eyes. "I would have. And I'll do the same if that's what we discover now."

His doubtful expression remained but he didn't argue.

"What are we going to do about Roth?" she asked.

He continued to stare at her. "What do you want to do?"

"Go talk to him."

Again, he stared at her. "What about Cullen?"

She didn't say anything. She didn't want to go behind his back but she didn't see any other way.

The elevator opened and Jag put his hand on her lower back, guiding her into the hall.

"I can't do this without you," she said.

"Yes, you could."

She smiled. "You'd only catch up to me."

He didn't return her smile. Instead, he opened their room door and let her in ahead of him. "Get the address to Roth's house. I don't want to meet him anywhere public."

Chapter 7

They waited until that evening to go to Colonel Roth's residence, and now they climbed onto the porch of a large Victorian house. Odie glanced around as Jag rang the bell. No one was lurking.

A few minutes later, a woman answered.

"Is Colonel Roth here?" Jag asked.

"Who are you?"

"Tell him we work for Cullen."

The woman eyed him and then Odie before closing the door. Odie looked at Jag.

"Is she going to get him?" she asked.

Before Jag could reply, the door swung open again and Colonel Roth's angry face appeared.

"What the hell are you doing here?"

"Sir, we need to ask you some questions."

He searched the front yard and street. "If there's anything you need to know, ask Cullen. You shouldn't be here."

"Please, sir, we just spoke with Frasier Darby's wife and she said he came to see you. It's important that we talk."

Roth opened the door wider and moved aside to let them in. He was a big man, a little thick in the middle, but not to the point of obesity. He wore glasses and his hair was gray and receding. Odie had never met him in person and seeing the man behind TES was awe-inspiring. Of course there were others he worked with to generate assignments, but the orders came from Roth. Odie didn't know any of the other members, only Cullen did, and it would stay that way.

Roth said nothing, just led them to a library off the dark wood floor and white trim entry. A white leather sectional faced a wall of windows and was flanked by towering bookshelves. Anytime she saw a library like this she admired the intelligence of its owner.

Roth turned to face them. "This better be good."

"We wouldn't have come if it wasn't important."

After a few seconds, he nodded.

"We need to know why Frasier came to see you," Jag said. "You didn't mention that to Cullen, at least, he didn't tell us when we started this assignment."

Roth ignored him. He stared at Odie and then something changed on his face.

"You're Odie." He sounded surprised.

He knew who she was?

"Odelia Frank?"

"Y-Yes…?"

Unbelievably, he smiled. "I knew your father very well. We were good friends. I don't know if you knew that."

"Uh…no." She looked at Jag and saw the shrug in his eyes.

"Most of our relations were on a professional level," he continued. "He was a good man. I never had a chance to say how sorry I am that he's gone, and I had to miss his funeral."

"Thank you." This was strange. Why was he talking about her father? As soon as he recognized her his temper had eased.

"I still can't believe anyone would want to kill him. And to think his killer was never caught..." Roth shook his head. "It's a travesty."

"I always wondered if it was someone on the inside. Someone who knew him," she said. Someone who wanted to silence him. She waited to see what Roth would say. Did he know anything?

"I can't imagine who. Your father was good at picking the best men. Whenever I needed someone, I always went to him first."

Realization expanded inside her head, catching her off guard. Cullen worked for Roth. Roth knew her father. "That's how Cullen found me." She said the thought out loud. "It was you."

"Yes. I asked Cullen to bring you home. And you went to work for him just as your father wanted."

"He never told me."

"Cullen needed a good intelligence officer, and I knew you had just resigned your position with the army. Your father was concerned about the state you were in after Sage was killed. I thought it was a good fit and he agreed. Cullen did, too. He was happy to have someone with your background."

Remembering that time sobered her. It seemed like another lifetime. She looked over at Jag. More so now than ever.

"Cullen says you're still trying to solve your father's murder," Roth said, bringing her back.

"Yes. Kate was helping me."

His brow creased in consternation. "I didn't know that."

No one did. Not until now. "I think she may have uncovered something that threatened his killer."

"But she was looking into Hersch."

"I know." She let him fill in the blanks on his own.

"You think his murder has something to do with this investigation?"

"Yes, but we don't know how." She explained about the initials and the package she never had a chance to fully study.

Roth lifted his hand and rubbed his forehead in thought.

"Why did Frasier come to see you?" Jag repeated the question, reminding them of the reason he and Odie were here.

Roth dropped his hand. "He knew I was close to Odie's father, but her father is dead, so he came to me instead. He's the one who told me Hersch was working with an Albanian military export company. I asked Cullen to validate the claim, given the fact that our government uses Hersch's services from time to time."

How did Frasier know her father?

"Why didn't you tell Cullen where you got the information?" Jag asked. "You could have saved us a lot of time. We could have looked into Darby earlier than now." She was a little angry about that.

"This began as a recon mission, and Darby begged me not to reveal his identity. My only concern at that time was to confirm his claim that Hersch was going rogue."

"But after Kate was murdered…" Odie said.

"Yes, after Kate was murdered everything changed. But by then I had Cullen on it."

So he hadn't intervened. He didn't want to stick his head out too far, not with TES involved. He didn't want his ties to the secret organization exposed.

"If we'd have known about Frasier Darby sooner, he might not be dead right now," Odie said, her tone sharp. She didn't care if he outranked her. Someone died because of his decision.

"I'm sure you'd like to believe that," Roth said.

He was right that she couldn't be absolutely sure, but his chances would have been much better had she and Jag known.

"Darby was afraid to approach us," Jag said.

"Because he didn't know who we were," Odie snapped.

"He was killed just a few days after Kate," Roth said.

"You should have told Cullen about him," Odie all but shouted.

Roth's eyes grew authoritative. "I don't think you fully understand what's at stake here. TES has grown into a formidable counterterror operation. Losing it would be devastating. But running an organization like that comes with a price. People die in this business. You should know that better than anyone."

She sucked her breath in. He meant Sage. And maybe even her father. "That's stooping a little low."

"So is coming to my home uninvited."

Odie clenched her teeth to bite back a caustic retort.

Jag cleared his throat. "How did Darby find out about the export company?"

Leave it to him to keep them focused on their purpose here.

Roth turned to him. "Someone told him about it, but he wouldn't say who."

"Why not?" Odie asked.

"He was afraid of detection."

"Was he afraid for himself or someone else?"

"He wouldn't say."

"And you didn't find that strange?"

"Don't forget he came to see me before Kate was murdered," Roth said.

She had to concede his intentions had begun on the up-and-up. Frasier hadn't wanted to reveal his sources because he was afraid. Roth hadn't questioned that. Maybe Odie wouldn't have either. She knew what it meant to protect her own contacts.

"How did he know my father? He's an engineer with no military ties." None that she could see.

"His brother was on the same team as Sage."

It felt like bomb had detonated inside her. "What?"

"That's how he knew your father. His brother was killed with Sage."

Was this all a weird coincidence? She looked over at Jag and saw his brow had lowered, and now he met her gaze intently, as if he were wondering the same thing.

"He must not have recognized you," Jag said to her. Frasier hadn't known she was Sage's wife, otherwise, he'd have probably approached them at the funeral.

"Do you think he talked to Kate?"

"It looks that way," Jag said.

Frasier had gone to Roth a month ago, before Kate was murdered, with information on Hersch. And then Kate had discovered more, something damaging enough to put her life in danger, something related to Odie's father's murder, as the initials on the package had indicated. Whatever she'd uncovered had led to Frasier's death.

Who was his source for the information on Hersch? Was it his lover? Kate?

No.

Frasier was a lot older than Kate and didn't fit the profile of a man who'd interest her. Calan was a handsome man. Much younger than Frasier, too. He was more her type. Odie wondered if he'd gotten involved with her on purpose. Maybe he discovered she'd done some digging and wanted to stop her. Except they'd known each other several months and had just moved in together. Hersch had only popped up on TES's radar a month ago.

Another coincidence?

Either that or all the players were closely tied together.

Frasier's brother had known Sage. Had their failed mission had anything to do with Hersch? It didn't seem likely. Nothing about Sage's death suggested foul play. It was only the common link that had led Frasier to Roth. It had to be. Frasier was out of his league and went to the only person he thought could help him.

"Why would someone like Frasier be involved in this?" Odie asked, trying to lure Roth into revealing what he knew about Frasier's lover. If he knew anything. "How does someone like that get his hands on information about Hersch? His source must have been his lover."

"What lover?" Roth asked, genuinely taken aback.

"Or someone who knew his brother," Jag said.

"Could be one in the same."

Jag nodded. "We need to find the lover."

"What lover?" Roth repeated, more insistent now.

"His wife told us he was having an affair just before he was killed," Odie told him.

"He never mentioned anything like that to me."

"He sounded sincere. How are we going to find her if we don't know who she is?"

Neither Roth or Jag had an answer.

"I'm sure the two of you can figure it out," Roth finally said. "You've been here too long as it is." He started toward the library entrance.

Jag put his hand on her lower back as they followed. Warm tingles distracted her from the thread of this evening's conversation.

Roth opened the front door. "From now on, all communications go through Cullen."

Odie nodded and preceded Jag outside.

"I'll get my report from Cullen," Roth said.

She glanced back with Jag at the colonel.

"Don't call me and don't come to my house again." Roth shut the door.

With a raised brow, she looked at Jag and he at her. He smiled.

"Nothing like a quick dismissal," he said.

"At least he talked to us." Not that they were any closer to solving this.

He put his hand on her back again and they walked toward the rental.

"He doesn't want to be discovered."

"Why do you think Frasier refused to reveal his source? Do you really think it was because he was afraid of detection?"

"Partly. If it were me, I'd want to protect my lover, too."

His voice was doing erotic things to her. Maybe it was his hand on her back. Maybe it was her earlier revelation that she'd grown more than she realized where Sage was concerned, and it was Jag who'd made her grow.

His hand slid down her back and brushed her rear. Odie stopped as sparks darted around her core. He opened the car door for her, standing close with a seductive grin.

"You did that on purpose."

"I've been dying to for a while now."

Was it her imagination or had he picked up on the change in her, too? She got in and watched his tall frame move around the front and get in on the other side. What happened to his lack of trust in her? Had telling him everything changed his attitude? That could be dangerous. Did she want to start something with him?

He *had* mentioned he wasn't going to do this kind of work much longer....

The next morning, Odie walked beside Jag after they left the elevator. They'd skipped dinner last night and now she was ravenously hungry.

"I want a big omelet with lots of cheese and spicy sausage."

"Potatoes, too."

Tilting her head, she smelled the air with a deep inhale. "I smell coffee."

"Stop that."

Seeing his heated expression, she straightened her head. Sharing a room had definitely tested their self-control last night. Odie was beginning to wonder if it would be so bad to just give in.

"You're making me hungry," he said, and it was clear he meant something other than food.

"Let's feed you, then."

"Be careful, or we won't make it through lunch."

The smile in his eyes gave her a warm tingle. There was promise in them, one that said he meant what he said.

"Stop being such a boy." She tried to make light of the undercurrent floating between them.

"Impossible around you."

So much for keeping it light. She couldn't believe it. They were talking about omelets and coffee and he was turning her on.

Clicking brought her head around. A cameraman was snapping pictures. What the…?

Then she saw the reporter from yesterday. He stood in the atrium in front of a cluster of trees, watching them pass.

"Odelia Frank?" he called.

Odie marched past him. As if she'd talk to him. Jag had taken into step behind her, blocking the cameraman's view of her. She could have kissed him for putting together what her picture in the paper could mean.

"Why did you go to Heather Darby's house yesterday?" the reporter shouted. She looked around and saw they were attracting attention. People looked from the reporter to her, his focus of attention and some of their expressions showed they were curious as to who she was. She didn't think anyone recognized her. It had been a few years since Cullen's daring rescue mission turned into a very public romance.

"I went back there after you went to Colonel Roth's house."

Odie stopped abruptly and slowly turned. Jag put his arm around her, his hand on her waist, no doubt ready to propel her away in a hurry if he needed to.

"Why did you go to see him?" the reporter asked, approaching them.

He came to a stop a few feet away. Odie didn't want to stay and talk to him, but this called for damage control.

"He's an old friend of the family," she said. Thank God it was the truth. "He knew my father."

The reporter gave her a plastic smile. "I spoke with

Heather Darby again. She said her husband went to see the colonel before he was killed. Any idea why he'd do that?"

"Why are you covering Frasier Darby's murder?" Jag asked.

"I'm sorry…who are you?"

"Another friend," he retorted.

Odie leaned against him and put her hand on his chest to make it look good. The reporter noticed and looked from Jag to her. She didn't think he was falling for it.

"Is he your partner?"

"He's my boyfriend."

That got Jag to turn his head, but it wasn't too obvious.

"You don't work with each other?"

"He came with me to look into Frasier's death."

"Isn't it more accurate to say Cullen sent you?"

Odie grunted her dismissal. "How would he do that with the media so hot for a new story about him?"

"I thought his company went out of business and he moved to some little mountain town to raise a family and sell mountaineering gear or something like that."

"That's true," Odie said.

"Or is that what you want everyone to think? Did he resurrect his company?"

"No."

"What would I find if I went to Roaring Creek and visited his shop?"

"Lots of mountain gear and small-town hospitality."

Odie saw him digest her sarcasm. "Where does he go when he's not selling ice picks and snow shoes?"

"Home to his wife and little girl."

The reporter sneered.

"Are you that desperate for a story? It would be a waste of airfare."

"What about you? Last I heard you moved from D.C. Do you live in Roaring Creek?"

"Who told you I moved?"

"Didn't you?"

"You think I'm going to tell you where I live?"

He'd never trace her to Roaring Creek. Odie stepped closer. She had to stop this man now or this would get out of control.

"The only story you're going to get is the one about Darby's murder. There's nothing going on, no secret mission, no cloak-and-dagger fascination, Jag and I are just here on personal time, trying to help out a friend."

The reporter laughed mockingly. "Personal time. Yeah, you two look like you're getting real cozy, but I'm not an idiot. I know you went to see Heather for a reason, and it has to do with her husband's murder. Someone with your background starts checking out the death of a nobody engineer, it makes me wonder if he isn't such a nobody after all."

"Frasier's brother was on the same mission as Odie's husband when they were both killed," Jag intervened. "That's how she knew the Darbys."

She could have kissed him again. He didn't have much to say but when he did it was well placed and clever. Though it was a risk giving even that much away, they had to make the reporter believe there wasn't anything to break open.

"You questioned Heather. She told me you said you couldn't tell her why Frasier came to you for help. She said you were investigating his murder."

Crap.

Crap, crap, crap!

"Why did Frasier go to you for help?"

"We can't divulge that," Jag said. "I believe that's what we told Heather, too, right, sweetheart?"

She looked from him and then the reporter. "Yes, darling, that's absolutely correct."

"Who is Calan Friese?"

"I wish we knew," Odie said. "Heather told us he came to her apartment after we left and asked why we were there."

"Do you think he's behind Darby's murder?"

"We don't know anything for certain. Beyond that, we can't comment."

The reporter studied them, taking in what she'd said. Then he asked Odie, "Are you working on behalf of the government?"

"No."

"If you'll excuse us," Jag said, "we were on our way to breakfast."

"What are you doing now?" the reporter asked, stopping them. "For a living, I mean."

"I'm retired."

"You're pretty young to be retired. McQueen must have taken real good care of you."

She didn't comment on that.

He took her in with his eyes. "It makes more sense that you'd continue doing the same work you were doing for McQueen. Whatever happened to his company? Security Consulting Services, I think it was called. SCS?"

"It's no longer a company. Cullen closed it and moved to Roaring Creek."

"Is he really running a mountaineering company? He doesn't seem like the kind of guy who'd be satisfied with something so...dull."

"What's so hard to believe about that? People age, they settle down. His marriage proposal was on national television."

He contemplated her and she thought she'd made some progress.

"Come on, Jag." She hooked her arm with his and they headed for one of the hotel restaurants off the atrium. She wasn't hungry now, though.

"I think I'm going to be sick," she said.

"I can't believe he saw us at Roth's."

Remembering how ga-ga she'd gotten over him when they'd left Roth's, she berated herself. She'd forgotten all about the reporter. She hadn't even thought to check.

"Me, either." She exchanged a little glance with Jag. They both knew damn well why neither of them had been aware of their surroundings.

Now she had her side pressed against him and it felt delicious.

There she went again. A reporter had just questioned her—seen her go to Roth's house—and all she could think of was sex with Jag.

A hostess seated them and Jag ordered for them both. She was too upset to concentrate on anything.

"Don't worry," he said.

"Aren't you?"

"No."

"Yeah, but you don't worry about anything." He didn't. He was always so calm. It was enviable.

"Cullen's going to blow a gasket."

"Yeah, he will."

Odie propped her chin on her hand and stared at the crowd of people in the restaurant. Waiters and waitresses hurried between tables. Couples chatted, families made too much noise.

How could he be so accepting of what would come? She didn't want Cullen to blow a gasket.

Their food arrived. Odie looked down with regret at her cheese-and-sausage omelet and the crispy potatoes on the side that were done exactly the way she loved them.

"Eat," Jag commanded.

She sent him a sullen look before picking up her fork and poking at her omelet. She cut a piece and moved it aside. Her stomach was upset.

Across the table, Jag shoveled a forkful of eggs Benedict into his mouth, chewed and swallowed and went for another bite. He sipped his coffee and caught her lack of interest in her plate.

Putting his cup down, he repeated, "Eat."

Reluctantly, she slipped her fork under the bite of eggs and put it into her mouth. She swallowed and lifted her cup of coffee. That was better.

She drank her coffee for a while.

Cullen was a good friend and the best boss she'd ever had. She didn't like the idea of letting him down. She'd already let him down enough. It didn't mean she was weak. This was all just too personal for her, not like any other mission. It wasn't business as usual.

"Odie."

His deep voice drew her up from her abyss a little. His tone held the hint of a teasing warning.

"Eat," he said again.

She looked at his eyes, amazed at how much she was beginning to like their green color and the way he let her see more every once in a while.

With a small smile, she tried a few more bites and made it halfway through her order. She even got some potatoes down.

Jag paid and they left the restaurant. She thought they were headed for the elevators until Jag put his hand on her back and steered her toward the exit.

"What are we going to do now?" she asked.

"Be tourists for the day."

She looked at him.

"That reporter is waiting outside—don't you think he isn't."

"I know." She hung her head. When Cullen found out about this, her job was finished. He'd turn his back on her and deny any association.

"I'll take care of you, Odie. Don't worry."

That sounded so sweet. Did he mean it?

"How would you do that?"

"I'm going to get your mind off everything. We need a break anyway."

He'd already begun to take her mind off everything but him. She watched him walk beside her, admiring his tall frame and impressive chest in a golf shirt that matched his eyes. He had on those holey jeans, too. What a combination.

"Where are we going?" she asked.

"We can't do anything until the reporter goes away. So, let's bore him with a trip to the National Mall."

Outside, she spotted the reporter. He and his cameraman were in a black sedan across the street, watching them.

"Can't we give him rat poison or something?"

He grinned. "That's my girl." He flagged a cab down and got in after her.

She stared out the window.

"He doesn't know enough, Odie," Jag said, putting his arm behind her on the seat. She turned to look at him, getting cozy in his arms. "So we went to see Frasier's wife. So we went to the colonel's house. They're close to the family. That's not a headline. It won't even make the evening news."

"He'll write something up."

"In the local paper. And it would be a boring story. The most he has is a mention of you knowing Frasier."

"What if he doesn't stop trying to follow us?"

"He can try all he wants."

Odie relaxed, her shoulders loosening a little. He was right. They hadn't paid attention before, but they would now.

The cab let them out and they crossed the street on the way to the Lincoln Memorial. Odie saw the reporter get out of another cab. He'd let his cameraman go but he wore a camera around his neck now. She faced forward before he saw her notice him.

Jag took her hand and she relaxed even more. Why not enjoy this while she could? It didn't mean she had to fall madly in love with him.

They walked among a throng of other people down a sidewalk. At the wide, steep stairs that led to the memorial, she stopped to look east across the reflecting pool at the Washington Monument in the distance. She'd been here many times before but each time revived her sense of purpose. She upheld what these monuments stood for, in a behind-the-scenes sort of way. She'd grown up learning the principles of freedom, and the cost of holding on to it. The Lincoln Memorial was her favorite, for all it meant to her. Humanity. Moral values. Unity. Freedom. Things that terrorists wanted to destroy.

She climbed the stairs with Jag. Inside the towering structure, she turned in a circle, taking in the words on the walls and Lincoln's giant stone figure.

"You look like him," she joked.

"I don't have a beard." He looked at her as if he thought she was serious.

She stopped herself from laughing. "No, I mean the stony part."

He moved toward her. "I prefer strong and silent." He glanced suggestively up at Lincoln.

Backing away, she laughed. He caught her in two strides.

Sliding his arm around her waist, he brought her against him. She wondered where the reporter was. Close by, she guessed, since Jag was putting on a show.

Or was he?

The way he looked at her made her uncertain. The chemistry between them was bubbling hotter.

Putting her hands on his chest, she slid them up and over his shoulders. She had to admit she was taking advantage of this.

"Odie," he warned in a deep voice. "Stop playing around."

"You started it."

"I'll end it, too. And not the way you might think."

"Sounds more like a promise than a threat."

Tourists milled around the open space of the memorial. Cameras clicked. Voices clashed and laughter rang. Children yelled and cried. But it all went into the distant background when Jag put his hands around her waist, holding her snugly against him.

"Now who's playing around?"

"I'm not playing," he said, and sank his fingers into her

hair. Odie tipped her head back and found herself staring into fiery green eyes.

No, he wasn't playing. And neither was she. Never before had she wanted a man to kiss her as much as she wanted Jag to right now. Not like this, with such quicksilver intensity. With Sage the attraction had taken more time to grow. At least she didn't remember it coming on this fast.

He angled his head a little as he brought his face closer. She could feel his breath. She closed her eyes when he came the rest of the way. The warm press of his mouth was different than on the day they'd had lunch at the Spicy Bowl. Urgency hovered on the brink of no control. If he deepened the kiss, they'd both be in trouble.

She pulled back first, aware once again of the swarm of people. He moved his arms from around her waist and held out his hand to her.

"Let's go to one of the museums."

She'd combust before this day was over. But she gave him her hand and they left the Lincoln Memorial. Outside, there was no sign of the reporter. No doubt he'd seen Jag kiss her and believed it was the real deal.

It was, and that gave Odie the wherewithal to endure the rest of the day with Jag without finding a cab and going back to their room so they could make love, instead of spending hours wandering through a museum.

By the time the cab pulled to a stop in front of their hotel, Odie was steaming hot. The reporter was long gone and she'd stopped worrying about being seen. She was more worried about how much she wanted to be alone with Jag.

He opened the cab door and extended his hand to her. Like all the other times, she gave hers to him. He helped her out of the car. She never let men do this for her, but somehow Jag doing it was appealing. She no longer thought of him as an operative. He was so different from her perception of one that it was impossible to keep him in the same league.

They entered the hotel and made their way around the tropical atrium, passing the checkout counter and stopping at the elevators.

When one opened, they joined two other women holding shopping bags and chattering quietly together. Jag's hand slid down to her rear.

Hot fire shot through her. Knowing they were on the way to the room only made it worse. There was no mistaking what he wanted. Maybe she shouldn't have come clean with him. He'd still be keeping his distance. But now he seemed to trust her, and that left nothing in the way of him pursuing her.

The elevator doors opened and the two women left. Odie backed up against the wall, forcing Jag to remove his hand from her. But she couldn't take her eyes off him. It was only three in the afternoon, but if she went to the room with him they were going to have sex.

"Maybe room service isn't such a good idea," she said.

"It's a great idea." His eyes were all smoky with desire.

The elevator doors opened. Odie hesitated before pushing off the wall. She wanted to pounce on him right there, wrap her legs around him and grind away.

He swept his hand in invitation to go ahead of him. She stepped out into the hallway. Each step closer to the room made her more breathless.

Was she ready for this?

She didn't have to marry him. She didn't have to pledge anything permanent with him, either. So what if they had sex. It would relieve tension. It was good exercise. So many good things...

She slid the card key into the door and opened it. Jag held it open as they entered. She heard it shut. The drapes were open and it was bright in the room. The bed was freshly made.

Facing him, she saw that he stood just a few feet from her.

"About today..." she started to say, but he tossed the rental keys on the desk and moved toward her. There was no mistaking his intent.

A flush of warmth sent her heart racing. She dropped the card key. His arm wound around her and he pulled her against him. He kissed her. His mouth moved over hers and then his lips opened and he marauded.

"Today drove me insane," he murmured.

"Me, too," she rasped.

Lifting his golf shirt, she ran her hands over his rippling skin. He lifted her shirt and pulled it over her head. Dropping it to the floor, he finished removing his own shirt and let it fall on top of hers. She just stood there and watched him. He unbuttoned his jeans but before he removed them, he reached around the back of her and unclasped her bra, kissing her as he did.

She kissed him back while he pulled the straps of her bra down her arms until it fell at their feet. He stepped back and sat on the bed to take off his boots. Odie sat next to him and took hers off. Kicking the second one free, she put her hands on Jag as he rolled on top of her, laying her down on the bed. Her feet still hung over the edge. He kissed her and ran his hands over her breasts, rising up to look at her.

He put his mouth over one nipple and Odie dug her head back against the mattress.

"I can't wait," he breathed. "Today was pure hell."

She had to agree. She watched him slide his jeans down, taking his underwear with them and kicking them to the floor. His thick erection jutted toward her. She wanted him inside her.

"Looks like heaven to me," she said.

"Lucky you." He unbuttoned her jeans.

"I'll be the judge of that."

He chuckled. "Shut that smart mouth of yours." He kissed her there while he pushed her jeans down.

"Or what?"

"Or…" Moving down to her throat, he kissed his way to the inner curve of her breast, making his way down to her stomach.

She moaned.

He pulled her jeans all the way off.

Climbing onto the bed, he straddled her on his hands. She spread her legs, her feet still hanging over the edge of the bed, and he put his knees in the space between. Holding onto his biceps, she watched his eyes as he put the tip of his erection against her and pushed. She felt stretched and tight, but she was so ready for him that he slid all the way in without any trouble.

"Heaven, for sure," she whispered. And then moaned again. It felt so good.

"Shh, or I'll tell everyone your mouth doesn't stop even during sex."

"Be careful, they might misunderstand you."

He chuckled seductively and slid his length almost all the way out of her and then pushed back in, bumping hips with her. He kept doing that, sliding in and out, excruciatingly slow. Odie had to close her eyes and groan.

Jag moved his arm under her and pulled her farther up onto the mattress. Then he hooked one of her legs with his arm, pulling it high and wide. Prickles of sensation rippled through her, building to delicious heights. She met his fiery eyes as an orgasm catapulted her into space.

Jag lay on her for a while and the significance of what had just happened descended on her. When she felt his body tense a little, she knew he was coming back down to earth, too.

He rolled off her and lay on his back. But Odie wasn't ready to face reality just yet. She rolled to his side and to her relief, he curved his arm around her. The energy between them was both something to celebrate and run scared from. They definitely were a pair in the sack, but where was this going?

She wasn't sure she'd be able to walk away from this, from Jag. And that was the frightening part. What scared her more was knowing Jag probably would agree. They both felt something powerful together. But even though Jag trusted her regarding this assignment, was he ready to trust her in love? And was she ready to take on love again? She was afraid the answer to both was no.

Chapter 8

Knocking jarred Jag from sleep. He lifted his head and looked beside him. Odie lay half on her side and half on her stomach, one leg bent and the other spread wide under the covers. Her hair partially hid her face, but he could see her full mouth and dark lashes outlining her perfectly shaped eyes.

He checked the clock beside the bed. It was late. After eleven. The evening with Odie rushed over him. After room service in bed, she'd crawled onto his lap and they made love that way, with dishes clanking and food spilling onto the comforter. Then after dozing for a while, he'd rolled her onto her back and gone a third round.

Another knock got him off the bed. Finding his jeans, he put them on.

At the door, he looked through the peephole. It was Senator Raybourne. Jag glanced back at the bed. Odie hadn't moved. But he figured this visit was too important to put off.

"Odie," he called.

She stirred, rolling onto her back and then propping herself up onto her elbows, looking sleepy and sexy, and very shagged.

"It's Raybourne," he said.

Wrapping the sheet around her, Odie woke up in an instant and trotted off to the bathroom.

Jag opened the door to a tense-looking Raybourne. But then Raybourne searched beyond Jag into the room with confusion.

"I thought this was Odie's room," he said.

"We're sharing one."

The senator sent him a startled look but quickly overcame the reaction.

"Come in. Odie will be out in a second."

Raybourne entered the room.

That's when Jag noticed he carried a file folder. "Something come up?" He already knew something had, or the senator wouldn't be here.

"Yes." He glanced toward the bathroom door when it opened and Odie emerged.

She adjusted the V of the white terry-cloth bathrobe so it covered more of her chest and then tightened the tie around her waist, seeming uncomfortable over the senator finding her in a room with Jag.

Up until now, he'd let down his guard with her. Nothing had come between them in bed, but maybe it should have. Maybe he shouldn't have let it go this far.

They'd had sex. Okay, so it was amazing. Fantastic. The best he could remember ever having…

That didn't mean she was the one for him. She had to feel the same and he had to be careful not to end up the one heartbroken when she couldn't give him what he needed. He didn't want to compete with a dead man. Just the uncertainty he felt with her should be enough to turn him away. He'd loved one duplicitous woman. He refused to be fooled again.

"Luis," Odie said in greeting.

"I'm sorry, Odie. I would have waited, but…"

"No. It's all right. What happened?"

When he extended the file to her, she took it. "What's this?"

"I received it today," Luis began. "There's a note inside from someone named Frasier Darby."

Odie opened the file. Jag moved to her side so he could see it, too. A handwritten letter was inside. Odie looked up at Luis.

"Who gave this to you?"

"Frasier's wife. Someone who didn't leave their name came to her apartment claiming he asked her to give it to me if anything happened to him."

Jag exchanged a look with Odie. Heather hadn't mentioned that to them, but Raybourne had said he hadn't received it until today.

"Frasier wrote about his suspicion of Kate's boyfriend," Luis said, "even going so far as to say he thought Calan was involved with Kate because he knew she was investigating your father's death."

Jag checked the date of the letter Odie had stopped reading to stare at Luis. Just last week. Had Frasier tried to go to Roth with this? Someone must have stopped him. Was that why he'd gone to the cabin? To hide? His wife had kicked him out, but why leave D.C. and go so far away?

"Calan knew my father?" Odie asked.

Luis hesitated. "Yes." The word sounded difficult to get out.

"How?"

Again, he hesitated. "This is going to be painful for you to hear, Odie."

Jag looked down at her and watched her press her lips together and then take a deep breath through her nose. But she pulled her emotion back in check, closing the file folder and holding her head high.

"Just tell us," she said.

Luis nodded. "Frasier began talking to Kate, who told him that Calan was working with someone named Dharr al-Majid. And that he was in Yemen when Sage's team was ambushed."

Jag caught Odie's subtle flinch. He felt like flinching, too. The last thing he needed after last night was to find out her father was, in fact, in cahoots with Dharr. And now possibly Calan.

"They were ambushed by rebels," Odie said, her voice more hopeful than certain.

"Yes. The team was supposed to have aided the Yemen government in a rebel uprising, but the rebels had already gathered and the team was outnumbered."

"That's what my father told me. They had bad intel going in."

"Very bad intel. Your father knew the rebels were tied to well-known terrorists, but he didn't know Dharr was leading them."

Jag's mind reeled. "Are you saying that Calan told Dharr about the mission?"

"Yes." Luis looked regretfully at Odie.

Her breath whooshed out of her. "No."

"I'm sorry, Odie," Luis said.

Although this supported her father's innocence, it

also meant Calan was behind the ambush that killed her husband.

She sat on the end of the bed. "Why?"

That was Odie. His brave Odie. Jag felt a surge of pride for her. This was hard on her but she was staying strong. He sat beside her anyway. At least she'd know he was there for her.

Luis sighed. "Calan didn't want his connection to Dharr exposed. Your father was close to figuring it out just before he was killed."

"But…"

Jag knew what she was thinking. Her father had met with Dharr. Calan had motive to set him up, but how had he arranged the meeting? Maybe her father hadn't known Dharr would be at the meeting place. And the email could have been easily sent from her father's computer by an intruder…to an untraceable email address. One not even Odie had been able to crack.

"According to Frasier, Calan was running arms for Dharr," Luis continued.

"All this time I…" Odie shook her head. "I never thought to consider that."

Odie hadn't heard what Luis said. She hadn't considered the possibility that Sage had been murdered. Who would?

Was Calan running the arms through Hersch and the Albanian export company? Luis hadn't said so it must not have been in the letter. If the letter was genuine. Call him a cynic but he always played on the pragmatic side. He needed his own validation.

"Why didn't my father tell me any of this?" Odie asked. "He knew about Dharr. The terrorists. The mission…" Her voice hitched.

"He didn't know until long after the mission. A year later. It's what got him killed. It's what got Frasier killed, too." He hesitated. "And Kate."

She fell into another lapse of thought, no doubt still reeling with the discovery that her husband had been murdered.

"Calan set it all up," she finally said, almost to herself.

It appeared that way. Jag still had some unanswered questions.

"Why did Frasier arrange for this to be sent to you?" Jag asked. Why not Roth?

"I don't know. Maybe because of the connection to Sage," Luis said. "Frasier's brother was part of the team and he knew I was close to Edward."

The senator must not know Frasier had gone to Roth. He saw Odie watching Luis, probably wondering about the same thing. Had Frasier learned something about Roth? Something that had made him turn to Luis?

"I'm so sorry, Odelia," Luis said. "I know this is going to be like losing Sage all over again. I saw what it did to you before. I shudder to think what knowing he was murdered will do."

Seeing her tear up, Jag felt a stab of apprehension. Odie was strong, stronger than any other woman he'd ever met and it was one of the things he liked about her most, but would she ever be able to overcome her loss and love another man the way she'd loved Sage? Once again he found himself backing away.

He didn't want to put his heart on a chopping block again. One too many times he'd misjudged the woman he was with, misjudged the relationship. And he'd come out of the experience with more to lose. Every time, particularly the last time, he'd invested more and felt more, believing that she felt the same. Either he was lousy at detecting the problem or he was too trusting. Well, not anymore.

He didn't have to ever forget her and how good it was with her, but he also didn't have to love her.

Odie lifted her eyes after staring at the folder to look at Luis. "It's been a long time. Sage is gone and I've accepted that. I've moved on." She sounded downtrodden and unconvincing. "I'll just be happy to see his killer behind bars."

"My father's, too," she added.

"They might be one and the same," Luis said.

Calan. Everything did seem to point to him. The way he met with Odie and didn't reveal anything, only fished for what she knew. The way he went after Frasier and possibly killed him. His wife's unsolved murder and the similarities to Kate's. Dharr. It all made sense.

But there were still so many unanswered questions. Why had Odie's father kept Calan a secret? What was Roth not telling them? And who was Frasier's lover? Three of many more he still had.

Odie yawned and stretched. They'd been parked in front of Hersch's sprawling two-level house for hours, and it was shaping up to be an uneventful night. Before coming here, they'd stopped by Heather Darby's house. She'd confirmed a man she didn't know had delivered the letter and asked that she pass it on to Senator Raybourne. What had Frasier learned that had stopped him from going to Roth? The answer was locked in Hersch.

She scanned the arms dealer's property from their vantage point across the street. There was no fence around his home, but it was on about a five-acre forested lot. Odie could barely see the structure through the maze of tree trunks and leafy vegetation. Hersch had two other houses, one in Florida, and the other in California. For a government contractor, he sure was loaded. She wondered how no one had noticed before now.

Jag rubbed his eyes beside her. Being with him was both a comfort and a bother. Aside from needing his support, she went from fighting urges to climb onto his lap to berating herself for allowing things to have gotten to this point. He'd withdrawn since Luis had left their hotel room. She hated that she couldn't enjoy the aftermath, savor the glorious feelings she'd had all day and into the evening. It had been a long time since she had felt as sated as that, or felt more deeply. Emotionally powerful. The way she'd felt with him overwhelmed her. With Sage it had taken more time to find that connection. They had spent more time getting to know each other before having sex. With Jag, it sprung up all at once, and led to gripping intimacy.

She didn't understand it and she needed to. Did he feel the same? Why had he withdrawn? The letter exonerated her father and pointed to Dharr as his killer. Yes, she'd destroyed the email and photo, but those had been planted to shift blame off Calan. He had no reason to not trust her now. Unless something Luis had told them opened his eyes. Something about Sage? It had to be obvious that she loved him. Did Jag wonder if his murder would prove too much for her? Maybe he wasn't comfortable going against the love she had with Sage. Maybe he was afraid he wouldn't measure up. His failed marriage made him skittish, that was for sure. So, let him be careful. She actually admired that about him. He wasn't going to dive headfirst into a relationship with her. She didn't want that, either.

How many times had she thought about this since they'd had sex? Every time she always circled back to what he'd said the night they were at the cabin, that he wasn't going to do this kind of work much longer, that he wanted to open a bakery. A bakery of all things. She smiled. She could see him doing that. He was another he-man that TES employed, but he was also…well…normal. A nice guy. And there was something sexy about a man whose masculinity wasn't threatened in a kitchen.

She leaned her head back on the seat and looked at him across the car. He turned to look at her, too.

"What are you smiling about?" he asked.

She didn't realize she was still smiling and she couldn't stop herself from asking, "Does your dad still run a bakery?"

It took him a few seconds to respond. She supposed, to him, the question had come out of the blue.

"No. He sold it and now he and Mom live in Denver. Retired."

"Really?" The idea of him having a close relationship with his family was another anomaly in her perception of him as a he-man op for TES.

"It's one of the reasons I agreed to work for TES. I could live close to them."

Her attraction to him grew a little more. She already knew he had a house in Denver. Why hadn't she thought of this before? Maybe she'd been too busy locking his operative side out of her heart to allow herself to care. Well, she cared now.

"Do you have any brothers and sisters?" she asked.

"A sister in Durango, and a brother in Dallas. They both have families."

She rolled her head to look through the windshield. Thinking of him at family gatherings, nieces and nephews climbing all over him, was charming. She'd never had many family gatherings. Her father had worked so much and she was an only child. Christmas had always been quiet. After the presents were opened and dinner was out of the way, her parents would sit and read. She'd get bored and go find her own thing to do. As an adult she'd spent the holidays either skiing or with military friends.

"Do you see them much?" she asked.

"Every year, at least. I talk to them on the phone, too."

The sound of his deep voice warmed her as much as his words. She was in danger of really falling for him. Unsettled by that, she focused on the driveway with an elaborate gate and guard shack. Every once in a while she spotted other guards patrolling the property. They were pretty regular. Predictable.

"What about you? Do you see your mom much?"

He pulled her back into the conversation. "Not really. She's always gone, traveling with friends or visiting them."

"It must be lonely as an only child."

She stared at him.

He grinned. "Cullen told me."

"Why were you talking about me?"

"I asked him about you once."

"Really." She already knew that, but she wanted to hear him tell her.

"Right after you gave me the cold shoulder. I was curious what made you that way. Didn't tell Cullen that, though."

"Being an only child didn't make me what I am today. My parents raised me well and I had a lot of friends. I wasn't lonely. It was the only way I knew. I don't know what it's like to have brothers and sisters."

"I know what made you what you are. I didn't when I first met you, but I do now."

Her father. Sage. He didn't have to say it for her to know that's what he thought.

A car turned into Hersch's driveway, stopping at the closed gate. The female driver slid her window down. The guard spoke to her through an open window in the guard shack and then nodded. The gate opened and the car drove up the long and curving driveway.

"How many is that now?" Odie asked.

"Four."

Two cars had arrived before this one, the first with two women inside, the second with one. Knowing Hersch's preferences, she wondered if they were here for sexual reasons.

"What kind of woman would want to get naked with three other women and one man?" she asked.

"One that gets paid to."

"I don't think these are hookers."

"Weren't you the one who said he paid them?"

"I said he probably had to."

"There you go."

She looked over at him and laughed briefly. He leaned comfortably back on the driver's seat, but he had to be anything but comfortable. They'd been parked out here for three hours. What was going on in there?

"Maybe he's having a midlife crisis," Odie said.

"You're assuming he paid those girls to come here."

"Of course he did." She'd studied his background.

He grunted. "You are Cullen's best."

At least he was on the same page as her. She stifled a smile. "You couldn't pay me enough to get naked with someone like him." Or any man for that matter.

"Me, either."

She laughed at the way that sounded and then they fell into a lapse of silence.

Across the street, the guard put his feet up on the console and opened a newspaper.

"Great," Odie said. "Hersch isn't going anywhere tonight."

"I figure we've got about two hours."

"To do what?"

He started the rental and began driving. "Go check out his office."

A little while later they drove past the nondescript building that was Defense Initiatives. The building looked to have once been an old warehouse. It was red brick with white trim and bars on all the windows, but tastefully done so as not to call attention. There were a few lights on, but it didn't look like he had much security here.

"Probably has twenty-four-hour security personnel."

"A guy behind a desk?"

"Yeah, and maybe one more to walk the property."

"Kind of odd for a man who does business with terrorists." In her experience the ones who didn't want to be noticed had something to hide. "This place screams front company."

"Yeah, that's what I was thinking. Government contractor by day, arms dealer by night."

He opened the car door and stood outside. Odie got out, too, and opened the backseat door. She bent over to dig into her work tote that was more of an equipment bag and found a keystroke logger. Jag was lucky she always came prepared. Tucking it into her pocket, she turned and saw him watching.

"Did you like the view?" She could tell by the heat of his eyes that he'd been staring at her butt.

"Yes."

"Stop that. We're working."

Grinning, he slipped on a pair of thin leather gloves and walked with her up and over an earthen berm separating the parking lot from the street. "What do you have in your pocket?"

"Something that will let us record Hersch's keystrokes. We'll know everything he does on his computer. I tried to send him an email with a nifty link to a Trojan but he didn't bite. Since we can't do this remotely, we'll have to come back to retrieve the data."

"I'll have to find another badge."

She looked at him askance as they walked down the other side of the berm and followed the edge of the parking lot. "You have one now?"

He pulled out a badge and held it up for her to see.

"I see you've planned ahead. How'd you get that?"

"I picked it up while you were with Friese."

"You just stopped by and picked it up, huh?" She shook her head. The man was amazing. "Does it get exhausting staying one step ahead of me all the time?"

"About as exhausting as it is for you to stay a step ahead of me."

"Not exhausting at all."

He grunted a laugh. "You made it easy on me. You had a list of Hersch's staff in the file you gave me. When I was on the way to the airport, I called each one through the main phone listing until I found one whose message said they were out. I found out where he lived and went there. His badge was on the kitchen table. He's a janitor."

"Glad I could be of help."

"You always are."

Scanning the roofline, Odie spotted what she was looking for. Two inconspicuous cameras, one on each front corner of the two-story building.

They stayed in the shadows at the edge of the parking lot until they made their way to the back of the building. Then Odie followed Jag up a ramp beside the shipping dock. There were no cameras here. Jag used his badge to unlock the double doors. Inside was an open shipping area full of worktables and shelves of boxes and a few desks sitting on a bare concrete floor. The dark globe on the ceiling had to be a camera. She and Jag slipped into the hallway off the shipping area.

Odie didn't see any cameras as they emerged into an area of cubicles. There were some stairs ahead. Hersch's office must be on the upper level. Better views there. Plus, there were no offices down here.

"If we were seen, we don't have much time," Jag said.

"You think?" she joked back.

They took the stairs. Upstairs was carpeted and had a lot fewer cubicles. Two or three conference rooms and a few offices. One had double wood doors and was in the corner of the building.

"That has to be his office," she said.

"Yeah." At the door, jag tried the knob. Locked.

"Of course," Odie said.

Jag took his badge from his back pocket and swiped the card reader beside the door. A clicking sound made Odie roll her eyes wryly.

"Janitor's badge," Jag pointed out.

"Or just more of your luck."

"Hey, whatever works." He entered the office ahead of her and she was careful not to touch anything with her ungloved hands.

Jag shut the door before he flipped on a light.

Slipping the keystroke logger from her pocket, Odie

went to the computer and leaned over the dual screens to reach the box behind them. She inserted the logger into a USB port and waited a few seconds. Then she removed it and tucked it back into her pocket. That's all she needed to do. The software would do the rest and Hersch would never know he had a little spy in his computer. God, she loved this part of her job.

Seeing Jag finger through a four-drawer file cabinet, she sat at the desk and plucked some tissues from a box Hersch had next to his computer monitor. There were two shallow drawers on each end and a center drawer. She opened the right drawer and found a few papers. She flipped through them. A couple of reports, and copies of invoices. She checked the vendors. Probably nothing notable. His center drawer was full of office supplies, all neatly compartmentalized in an organizer.

"Tidy," she said.

Jag glanced over at her as he searched a bookshelf adjacent to the desk. He returned his attention to pulling out books and looking behind them, as if he were looking for a hidden switch.

Smiling, she opened the left drawer. All that was in there was a pistol and some ammunition. A Ruger SR9. Could do better.

Hearing voices outside the office, she looked up and stared at the door. If the security guards had seen them on their monitors and were looking for them, maybe they didn't think they could get into this office since the doors were locked.

She looked at Jag.

"Are you ready?" he whispered.

Nodding, she got up and stopped behind him. He turned off the light and opened the door a crack. Quiet.

They slipped out. Jag took her hand and led her through the carpeted area. Odie saw a guard appear from inside an office and another one emerged from the stairs.

Jag pulled her into a dark conference room, standing between her and the door against the wall.

"Have you seen anything?" one of the guards asked. "I saw them come in through Shipping."

"No, but they're using Enrique's badge. They can get into any office."

"That's all we need—somebody breaking into Hersch's."

"Let's go check all the offices."

"We should call the cops first."

"Are you nuts? Hersch said no cops."

Odie barely heard that last snippet as the guards made their way to the other side of the building.

"I need to get to the security desk," Jag said.

Still holding her hand, Jag pulled her from the conference room. She let him lead her toward the front of the building. Behind the security desk, Jag began opening drawers. He found a visitor badge and started keying into one of the two computers' security software. A minute later, he was finished. He'd used the number on the badge to code it into the system. If no one noticed the missing badge, it would be easy to return.

Taking her hand again, Jag once again led her through the building. She thought it was odd that she didn't mind his protectiveness. She could certainly take care of herself, but she liked her hand in his. They ran down the stairs and through shipping. Outside, he pulled her toward the edge of the parking lot.

"Hey, you!" one of the guards yelled.

Odie saw him coming from the front entrance.

"Stop right there!"

She stumbled as Jag ran faster. He had longer legs than her.

"Run faster!" he yelled.

"I'm running as fast as I can!" She glanced back to see the guard trying to catch up to them, but he was short and stocky and was losing ground.

Up and over the berm at the edge of the property, she ran down the other side with Jag. He let go of her hand and she scrambled to get into the rental. He peeled rubber racing away. Odie looked back and saw the guard with his hands on his hips, heaving breaths of air and watching them drive away. But she wasn't foolish enough to think they were in the clear.

Chapter 9

Odie woke facedown on her pillow. One of her legs was outside the covers and her skin felt chilled. She lifted her head. "Ugh." Rubbing her eyes, she rolled onto her back and propped herself up by her elbows, trying to blink the sleep from her eyes. She'd slept hard.

Jag came out of the bathroom in only his boxers. That woke her up. His ripped abdomen sloped to a white cotton waistband, the roomy material only hinting his treasures. His hair was still wet from his shower.

He bent over his bag, eyeing her with what she could only call annoyance. She frowned.

"It's about time you woke up," he said grumpily.

"What time is it?"

"Twelve-thirty."

"Stop keeping me up every night then," she said.

"That wasn't all me."

He sounded resentful, and he was alluding to their night

together. What was the matter with him? They'd gotten along fine last night.

"What's got you so grouchy this morning?" She flung the covers off her and got off the bed. She'd put on her sleeveless cotton Shrek pajamas before falling asleep. He watched her grab some clothes from her bag.

"It's *afternoon*." He glowered at her as he put on another pair of faded, holey jeans. "I've been awake for hours."

She held some jeans and a blue button-down stretch shirt against her and faced him. "So?"

"So, your butt was sticking up the whole time and your legs were spread and one of them was outside the covers." He extended his arm toward the bed as he spoke. Or yelled was more like it.

His body language screamed his frustration. She almost laughed. "You watched me sleep?"

"I had the TV on."

She glanced at the television. It was playing so low she could barely hear it. He'd been careful not to wake her up, but watching her sleep had driven him mad.

"Poor baby."

"I'm not in the mood for your mouth today."

"Are you just bent out of shape because we had sex?"

He yanked on a golf shirt and didn't respond.

"Why didn't you wake me up and just take me?" He'd be in a better mood.

He scoffed as he straightened his shirt. "Unlike you, I'm not in denial over what happened."

Denial? That threw her for a second. "Don't make a big deal over it." But inwardly she was afraid it was a big deal. She was afraid to put too much importance on it.

"Exactly what I mean."

She stared at him. Did he think it was a big deal?

Uneasiness crept over her. She liked the idea of him feeling that way.

Her cell phone started ringing.

"Saved by the bell," she quipped, dropping the clothes to answer it.

"Odie."

It was Cullen. Her stomach flopped and she stopped breathing for a second.

"You'll never guess who just called me," he said.

She remained quiet, but sought out Jag with her eyes.

"What did I tell you about going to see him?" he demanded. She didn't think she'd ever heard him so angry before.

"Not to go," she answered. No point in making excuses.

"And what did you do?"

"I went."

"Yes, and not only did you go see him, you brought Jag with you, which means you told him what I asked you not to."

It did look bad. Really bad. But if they didn't check out every lead, they might never expose who was behind all this. "Cullen, I'm sorry, but you have to try and understand—"

"The only thing I need to understand is you aren't following orders. I got my ass chewed because of you."

Odie held her silence. Roth had been angry they'd showed up, but she'd hoped his friendship with her father would have smoothed the edges enough.

Jag came to stand in front of her, watching her and listening.

"He's pissed," she mouthed.

"Did anyone see you go there?" Cullen asked, and Odie closed her eyes.

After a long hesitation, she didn't have to reply.

Cullen swore three times and she heard a bang, as if he'd pounded his fist on his office desk.

"Who?" he growled.

Opening her eyes, she met Jag's intent gaze. "A reporter. The same one who recorded you saying you wanted to marry Sabine after you rescued her from Afghanistan."

That rendered Cullen speechless. She could only imagine what was going through his head.

"I can't believe this," he finally said, and the disappointment she heard broke her heart.

"Cullen." She had to try to defuse him. "He doesn't have anything to go on. We played it like we knew Frasier Darby because his brother was on Sage's team when they were both killed, and the colonel was close to my father. Which is the truth," she emphasized. "He thinks we're looking into Frasier's death."

"He's going to be watching you."

"Then let him. He won't find anything."

Another long silence passed.

"After all the years we've worked together," he finally said, "I thought I knew you, Odie. Now you pull something like this. I don't even know what to say to you."

"Put yourself in my shoes for a minute. My father was murdered and this is all connected. Hersch. Kate. Frasier. And whether you agree or not, Roth."

When he didn't respond she asked, "What would you have done?"

"I don't know, but I do know I never would have betrayed you."

The sting from that came at her in a giant wave. She never meant to betray him. "I'll send you a report of everything we have so far…including the reason I came to D.C. without Jag."

"It's too late for that. You and Jag are both suspended until further notice."

That hit her with a dagger-sharp blow. "What?"

"I'll assign someone else to Hersch. If you want to investigate your father's murder, do it on your own dime."

She should have known he'd react like this. Maybe she did and it hadn't mattered. She'd have gone no matter what. With or without Jag.

"That's a little harsh," she said.

"I don't have a choice. If that reporter finds out you still work for me, TES is finished. Think about that."

He was right. Some day the reporter might come to check on Cullen and find her working at his shop.

"All right. We're suspended, but Hersch had something to do with my father's murder, so don't send anyone else to tail him."

As Jag listened, he shifted his weight on his feet while his brow lowered ominously over his eyes.

"And I'm sending you a report whether you like it or not."

"Fine. Arguing with you is always useless. Send the damn report, just don't let that reporter get any closer than he already is. And don't let him trace you here. That above all else, Odie. You follow me?"

"Yes." She'd move hell to heaven trying, anyway.

After she disconnected, she looked up at Jag.

"Suspended? Really." Sarcasm dripped from his tone.

"Roth called him."

He sighed hard and shook his head in frustration.

She wondered if he was thinking this would never

have happened had he not been attracted to her. Was she dragging him down a cesspool of her own creation?

"Jag...I'm sorry."

He met her eyes and she sensed his mood soften. "You didn't force me to go with you."

"No, but..."

"I wouldn't have done anything differently, Odie. Too many people have been murdered because of this. It's time to put an end to it."

She wasn't convinced. What about his reticence over being with her?

"And I wanted you to tell me about Roth."

In his eyes she could see his meaning. Not only had she trusted him enough to tell him, she'd told him the truth. She was being straight with him now, and that had gained his respect. Her heart melted all over itself. He was on her side. All the way.

She threw her arms around him and kissed him. "Jag."

The only thing he didn't trust her with was his heart. Well, she didn't trust herself with her own heart and right now she didn't care.

He slid his hands around her back, scrunching up her Shrek pajamas. He pulled the hem up and put his hands on her hips, groaning when he discovered she hadn't put on underwear.

Leaning back, she tugged his shirt up his chest. He lifted it over his head while she went for the button of his jeans.

He took the task over for her. "Take that girly nightshirt off."

Smiling, she complied, lifting it over her head. Standing naked before him, she waited while he stared at her and finished removing his jeans. When he did, he still looked at her. She loved it, his passion, his appreciation. Stepping closer, he reached out and touched her breasts. His fingers felt like warm butter gliding over her sensitive skin. She closed her eyes and let her head fall back a little, basking in the glorious feelings he set afire. She didn't move to touch him back, just let him take his time enjoying what he was doing. He moved closer. She felt the heat of his body, and the brush of his hardness on her belly.

His hands slid down to the curve of her waist. She watched him watch what he was doing, sliding over the curve of her hips to her butt, where he gently squeezed. Now his eyes met hers. She was fire for him. She put her hands on his muscular chest and slid them up until she looped her arms around his shoulders.

He kissed her, soft and slow.

Oh. This was beyond anything she'd experienced.

"What are we doing, Odie?" His breath warmed her lips and face.

She kissed him, not wanting this cloud of pleasure to fade. He kissed her back, harder now.

"What are we doing?" he asked again.

"Just make love with me, Jag. I don't want to think about anything else."

He pressed his lips to hers again.

"Just this." She kissed him back.

Holding her around the waist, he stepped forward and she stepped back until she felt the edge of the bed. Scooting back on the mattress, she stretched her length on it, bending one arm over her head.

Jag looked at her for timeless seconds before kneeling on the mattress and coming down on top of her. He braced her head between his hands and kissed her again, deeper and more urgent now. She slid her hands down his back, feeling his muscles ripple with movement as he propped his weight up on his hands. She opened her legs and pulled him closer.

Her gaze locked with his as he found her and penetrated. Love swelled inside her as he pushed in all the way. His breathing went in tune with his movements. Back and forth. But it wasn't enough.

"More," she rasped.

He pushed harder. Still it wasn't enough. She couldn't get enough of him.

"Jag."

With a growl he slammed harder, moving his hips in a grind. That sent her over the edge with a yell.

Rolling onto his back, he took her with him and lifted her. She straddled him, still reeling from sensation, and he guided her onto him. Her mind went numb. She put her hands on his chest and met his eyes while he thrust upward. She held herself above him and then met his rhythm. He groaned deep. She ground her hips against him and coherent thought once again took a spiraling nosedive.

When awareness finally returned, Odie leaned down and kissed Jag's mouth. His eyes were lazy with satisfaction. She kissed him again, and then kissed the corner of his mouth when it curved in a soft smile.

Oh.

Her heart burgeoned with emotion she was too afraid to name. Sliding off him, she lay next to him. He held her sweetly. It so overwhelmed her that she closed her eyes.

"Stop it," his deep voice said.

"I'm not doing anything."

"You're thinking too much."

"Then you must be, too."

After a few breaths, he said, "I am."

* * *

Around dinnertime, the room phone rang.

Jag turned his head to see Odie, whose head was still cradled comfortably in the curve of his arm. She opened her eyes, a smile shining in them. He just about turned into a pile of love-struck mush at the feet of a beguiling woman. Except beguiling didn't have the right ring for a woman like Odie. Demanding. Even in bed. But he'd satisfied her. Smiling back at her, he slid his arm free and sat up.

"I hope this doesn't always happen," she said.

He loved how she said things the way they were. This was the second time they'd been interrupted in bed.

The phone rang a third time and he reached over to pick it up. "Yeah."

"It's Calan Friese. I'm in the lobby. Meet me at The Cure in ten minutes." And then he hung up.

Jag hung up the phone and turned to Odie. "Friese is in the lobby. He wants us to meet him at The Cure."

Her eyes lost their dreamy slumber and she flung the covers off her. He got a magnificent sight of her beautiful backside as she went to her bag and dug out some clothes. He propped himself on one elbow and watched her profile, firm breasts jiggling as she hurried.

She caught him looking. "Get up." She threw her underwear at him. It hit his face and fell to the mattress.

Taking it in his hand, he stood and went to her. Handing her the underwear, he leaned over her shoulder and kissed the corner of her mouth. She turned and slid her arms over his shoulder and kissed him fully.

"Careful, or we'll be late."

Laughing, she let him go and slipped on her underwear. Reluctantly, he dressed with her.

Jag took Odie's hand as they entered the restaurant. High

ceilings and oak and stone walls made it inviting. Tall oak stools lined a glass-topped bar.

Calan sat in a booth with a black-topped table near the entrance. Jag sat on the opposite bench first, and then Odie sat beside him.

"The police are looking for me," Calan said, meeting Odie's eyes in an accusatory way. Jag found that interesting. He sounded annoyed more than afraid—not worried that the police wanted to question him.

Odie didn't seem to notice. "Maybe you deserve it."

"Maybe I don't," he shot back. "Who have you been talking to?"

Odie didn't respond.

"I know you're the reason the cops are after me," he said.

"It was you who told Dharr about Sage's mission," Odie said. She was more emotional than Jag was accustomed to seeing her. "Not my father."

Calan went still and just looked at her.

"He knew something, didn't he?" Odie charged. "And you didn't want him to talk."

"You have your facts wrong. It was *your father* who betrayed the mission to Dharr. You of all people should know that."

"I don't know anything of the sort."

"You're the one who buried key evidence. That email and the photo? This would have been over a long time ago if you hadn't done that. Kate would still be alive, and so would Frasier."

Kate must have told him about the email and photo.

"Kate believed in my father's innocence as much as I did," Odie said.

"Yes, and that's what we fought about the night she was killed."

"You mean the night you went *driving*?" Odie taunted.

"She refused to believe me and she defended you for hiding clues to the truth." Calan turned to Jag. "Edward Ferguson was dealing arms with Dharr, and Sage must have uncovered it. That's why Edward told Dharr, so Dharr would be waiting to ambush the team."

Calan believed Odie's father was guilty because of the email and photo, yet Frasier's letter suggested something entirely different. Which was true?

"How do you know about the mission?" Jag asked.

"I was there. I was after Dharr. By the time I finally caught up to him, he and his men were attacking the team. But he didn't know I was there. Nobody did. Except for Sage. He'd already been hit so I dragged him away from the attack. Before he died, he said Dharr knew they'd be there and that it was Hersch who betrayed them. Hersch and someone else. He said there had to be someone else."

"That's a lie!" He'd spoken with Sage? He was there when he died? It was too much.

"Your father didn't know I was there, either. I kept it that way so that I could do my own investigation."

Odie scoffed. "You were working with Dharr. It wasn't my father, it was *you*. You're the one who killed Sage!"

"I didn't kill anyone. Who told you that?"

She didn't answer. It was her customary response. Never reveal a source. But in this case, it needed to be revealed.

"It was Senator Raybourne," Jag said, earning a glare from Odie.

But he got what he was after. Calan's reaction said it all. Few things shook Jag, but this stopped him short.

Calan breathed an incredulous exhale and leaned back

against the booth seat, shaking his head. Jag waited for him to explain the revelations going through his head.

At last Calan looked at Jag. "Did he have proof?"

"Yes. A letter from Frasier Darby," Odie said smugly.

The letter was pretty damning, but Jag had a feeling Calan would dispel most of his doubt by the end of this meeting.

"Who sent him the letter?"

Odie hesitated.

"Someone gave it to Darby's wife to give to Raybourne," Jag said for her. Luis hadn't known Frasier had gone to Roth, and Roth had told him and Odie the truth.

Calan grunted derisively. "He could have paid someone to deliver a forgery to her."

"It wasn't a forgery," Odie said.

"It had to be since I'm not doing business with Dharr and I had nothing to do with the ambush."

Jag understood her loyalty to an old family friend, but it was clouding her judgment. The same had happened when she'd destroyed evidence. Planted or not.

"You murdered Frasier," Odie said. "We saw you there."

"No, Raybourne was behind that job. I got there right after it happened, just like you."

Jag nodded. "Nice work on the brakes, by the way."

Calan turned to him while Odie continued to radiate animosity. "I didn't want you to follow me. I knew what you'd think, that I killed Frasier and Kate, but I didn't. Raybourne did. I didn't know it then, but I do now. It had to be him."

Odie stood from the booth. "Luis wouldn't have done anything like that! You're just trying to shift blame."

The couple seated at the booth behind Calan turned to see what was going on.

"No, he didn't do it himself, he hired someone to do it for him." Calan kept his voice low. "Someone professional."

"This is ridiculous. Jag." She looked pointedly at him. "Let's go."

"Calm down, Odie."

"Calm down? Listen to what he's saying. You met Luis. Do you think he's capable of anything so vile? His own stepdaughter, for God's sake!"

He'd only met the senator a few times. He didn't know him. But people backed into a corner sometimes turned to drastic measures. "You're being irrational, and it's not like you." In fact, he doubted anyone had ever seen her like this. So shaken. He felt for her but this was too important to back down now.

"Raybourne tried to make Edward take the fall," Calan said, "but you destroyed the evidence he planted. The case went cold, lucky for him, until someone got suspicious. So he's doing it again, only this time it's me he'd like to fall."

"You don't know that," Odie said.

"I do now. I thought your father was the one who ambushed that mission, but all this time it was the senator. No wonder it's taken this long to figure out."

"No," she shot back. "Why would he do that? What reason would he have? He's a good person with high moral standing."

"And maybe he's also a good actor."

Odie all but steamed anger. "Luis wouldn't have murdered his own daughter. And my father…it's…unthinkable!"

Again, the table next to them fell silent.

"Kate was his stepdaughter," Calan countered. "Not his biological daughter."

"That doesn't matter. He raised her. They were close."

"Then whatever he's in on, it must be huge. He's finished if it gets out."

"He's on the U.S. Senate Arm Committee," Jag pointed out.

Now Odie looked injured when she turned her eyes to him.

"Convenient," Calan said.

"Especially for Hersch."

"Jag." Odie sounded hurt.

It was unpleasant for him to force her to face this, but it all made perfect sense. He ignored her. "How did you meet Kate?"

"At a barbecue," Calan answered. "Colonel Roth invited me. Kate was there with Raybourne and his wife."

Jag heard Odie's sharp inhale. "You're lying."

"I used to report to Roth," Calan continued without acknowledging Odie. "I quit after my wife was murdered and that mission fell apart. Something like that has a way of souring a man's loyalty to our country's defense organizations."

Because he thought Edward had arranged to have those men slaughtered. Odie's husband. Jag looked up at her where she still stood by the table, staring at him. He could tell she was fighting tears. It had to be difficult to absorb. Sage. Her father. Kate. All of them killed because of the senator, a close family friend.

"Raybourne didn't know I knew Sage," Calan went on. "If he had, I doubt he'd have allowed me to be with Kate. She was always helping Odie. It didn't come up until she told me about that photo and the email. That's when we started disagreeing. I thought Edward was behind it all and she was on Odie's side. And then Odie destroyed the evidence."

It explained why he hadn't trusted Odie when they'd met.

"I told her about Dharr," Calan said.

"Is that when she sent Odie the file?"

"She never discussed her dealings with Odie in detail, especially after we started disagreeing, but yes, I'm sure she included everything about Dharr. She may have even included her speculation that if it wasn't Odie's father behind the betrayal, who could it be?"

Someone in a powerful position. Someone who'd be able to grease the way for an arms dealer like Hersch.

"How do you know Dharr?" Odie asked, uncharacteristically shaken. "Why are you after him?"

When he looked at her, his eyes changed to reveal grief. "I married a woman who was with him when I met her. After he found out we were together, he killed her."

That made Odie stiffen. Calan's wife had her throat slit. Just like Kate.

"So you've been after him ever since."

Calan's certain nod said he wasn't stopping until Dharr was dead. "But he's good at staying hidden."

"They usually are." Terrorists were like rats that way.

"I don't believe this."

Jag looked up at her the same time Calan did. He was beginning to worry he'd been wrong about her. What would she do to protect Luis? She hadn't believed her father guilty and look what she'd done. Would this time be any different?

"Sit down, Odie," he told her.

"No. We're finished here. Don't you see what he's doing?"

Jag just stared at her. Was she really turning a blind eye?

"We need to talk about how we're going to proceed," he said.

"You and I can do that." She sent Calan an abhorrent look.

"He can help us."

"No, he can't. Jag. Come with me to the room right now."

"No."

"Then I'll do this myself."

"Do what? Hide evidence? Warn Luis?"

She sucked in another sharp breath. "You think I'd do that?"

"You've done it before and you're acting weird right now. You know what Calan is saying is true. You just aren't accepting it."

"More like you don't want to trust me," she retorted. "You think I'm going to go do something illegal."

"Actions speak louder than words."

"What?"

"Sit down."

"Go to hell." With that she turned and marched out of the restaurant.

Jag sighed. He was going to have to track her down again.

"Let me guess. You slept with her."

Chapter 10

"Wait for me." Odie trembled as she climbed out of the cab. The evening air was warm and a little humid and the sky was clear.

All the way here she'd been drowning in thoughts. Horrible thoughts. Coming at her from every direction.

That last day with Sage. Sending him off to a mission that was doomed from the start, if she believed what Calan said. And her father hadn't known. That should come as a relief. He hadn't sent Sage to his death. But the senator had. And when her father discovered it, Luis had him killed.

But how had her father learned what the senator was doing? Sage? Maybe Sage hadn't known enough but was getting too close, and it had taken her father a year to connect the dots and add a few of his own.

Oh, God. Her heart felt crushed in her chest. Sage must have known enough to threaten the senator the morning he'd left for his mission. Only Sage hadn't realized it. Had her father talked to the senator about it? Maybe gone to him for help, knowing Dharr was buying arms? Maybe her father had grown suspicious of Luis who led him to Yemen and then arranged for Dharr to send the email and kill him.

She wiped a tear that had fallen from her eye. She hadn't even been aware that she was crying. She was in such a daze.

She rang the bell of Senator Raybourne's home, a huge modern sprawl in an upscale neighborhood of Alexandria. Nothing a man of his position couldn't afford, and nothing that suggested he made lots of money helping to channel arms to terrorists.

She caught her breath with the thought, it stabbed her so deep.

His wife opened the door. "Odelia?"

"Hello, Alice. Is Luis home?"

"He ran out for a dinner with some colleagues but he should be back within the hour. What's wrong? You look like you've been crying."

Odie wiped her face again. "Sorry. I…" She looked at the woman, whose worry was conveyed in her eyes. "Can I talk to you about something?"

"Of course." She opened the door wider and Odie stepped inside. Alice led her to a tastefully blended cream-and-earth-toned sitting area that opened off the entry. High ceilings made the brick gas fireplace tower over the room.

Odie sat on the cream-colored leather sofa and Alice sat in the chair adjacent to her. A ticking grandfather clock was the only sound, that and the soft hum of a refrigerator.

"Luis told me that Sage's mission was set up to be a trap," Odie began, waiting for Alice's reaction.

The woman sat straighter and stared with wider eyes at Odie.

"Didn't he tell you?"

"N-no. Oh, Odelia. That's awful! When did you find out?"

"Just yesterday." She explained about Dharr and Calan and finally her father, all the while watching Alice.

"Did Luis tell you any of this?" Odie asked.

"I was with him when Kate came to talk to him about the man named Hersch. She said she was looking into something for you. We were both so worried about her." She shuddered. "It sounded so dangerous."

Did Alice believe the senator? Odie wondered if she should tell her about her meeting with Calan and Jag. Then she realized how much her emotions had compromised her. Coming here may have been the stupidest thing she'd ever done. What would the senator have done if she had confronted him? He'd already killed Sage, his stepdaughter, Odie's father and Frasier. What would stop him from killing her?

Her heart wrenched with grief and she had to lower her head. Did she really believe Luis was capable of that? It didn't seem possible. Not real.

"Are you all right?"

Odie looked up at Alice. "I don't think it was Calan who leaked information about Sage's mission."

The abruptness of her declaration caused something to cross Alice's eyes. She looked scared for a split second. And her long hesitation made Odie wonder if there was something she wasn't saying.

"Why do you think that?" she asked.

Odie grew acutely alert. "There are some things I can't tell you." Like about Roth. "But Luis showed me a letter that a man named Frasier Darby wrote." It was a shot in the dark.

The scared look intensified. Odie stopped breathing for a second. Alice recognized Frasier's name. Could it be…? Was Alice Frasier's mysterious lover?

"Do you know him?" Odie asked.

"What are you going to do, Odelia?" Her voice trembled.

She must know him. "What do you mean, 'what am I going to do'? I'm going to find whoever killed Sage and my father and Kate and make them pay." Or kill them. For the first time since her husband died, she wanted to have her hands around the handle of a really big gun.

But would she be able to kill Luis? A man she'd known almost her entire life? A close friend to her father? Someone she'd trusted without reservation.

"Odelia, you should just let this go," Alice said imploringly. "Let the police handle Calan."

"Let it go?" That wasn't part of her fiber. And hadn't she just said she didn't think it was Calan who was responsible for all this?

"Too many people are dead. Stop now before it gets you, too."

"Do you know Frasier Darby?" Odie pressed.

Alice only stared at her, a struggle in her eyes. And then she relented. "He was someone I met at a veterans memorial fundraiser."

"Did you have an affair with him?"

Her hesitation gave her away.

"Does Luis know?"

Tears bloomed in her eyes and she crumbled. "Yes. He followed me one day, when I met Frasier at a coffee shop. He confronted me that evening and I told him everything.

He wasn't happy. I broke his heart." She paused as emotion choked her up a little. "He was very upset."

Odie was sure Luis had been upset about more than her affair. "When did he find out about the two of you?"

"Almost two weeks ago."

After Roth had contacted Cullen, but before Kate had been killed. "And what happened?"

"I agreed to stop seeing him."

"Did you?"

"After Kate was murdered, he came to see me a couple of times." She looked down, a woman in love without her lover. "But I haven't seen him since."

She must not know he was dead. "Did you tell him about what Kate was looking into?"

She nodded.

"He asked a lot of questions. He wanted to know why Kate would go to someone like Luis for advice. He didn't like Luis." Alice turned a bashful look toward Odie. "Understandably so."

Odie was sure there was more going on here. Had Kate's revelation about Hersch alerted Frasier to something? It must have, or else why would he go to Roth?

"Did Frasier know that Luis and Colonel Roth were friends?" Luis and Alice had gone to a barbeque at the colonel's house, one Calan had attended with Kate.

"Yes. Frasier knew Colonel Roth. He couldn't let go of his brother's death and Roth was close to your father. He talked to him about his brother. Frasier was afraid something had gone wrong on the mission and if anyone could help him, he believed Roth could."

No wonder why she'd looked so alarmed when Odie told her Sage's mission had been sabotaged. Odie's mind spun. Frasier must have been suspicious of Luis before Kate had revealed what she knew about Hersch. But he hadn't told anyone. Had he lined up with Alice deliberately? Is that why he'd kept his suspicions a secret?

"Why didn't you say anything?" If Alice knew Sage's team had been betrayed…

"I thought Frasier was only having trouble dealing with his grief. He had no real proof that anything went wrong."

That she knew of. Alice hadn't wanted to believe anything had gone wrong. She had her affair to hide. "Did Frasier ever talk to Kate?"

"No, I don't think so. But when I mentioned that Calan was her boyfriend, he said he'd heard the name before."

Frasier's brother was on Sage's team. They both reported to her father. And her father knew Roth. It made sense.

Frasier must have gone to Calan, but not before he'd told Roth about Hersch. Otherwise Roth would have known about Dharr. And if Calan had warned Frasier about Odie's father, he may have lost trust in Roth, who was close to Luis. He must have felt he had no one to turn to, no one to trust. Going up against a colonel and a senator all on his own, an ordinary engineer, he had good reason to be cautious. He probably hadn't trusted Calan, either, who to him must have seemed like an ex-Delta soldier gone rogue.

"Alice, how much do you know about what Luis is doing aside from his role on the arms committee?"

"What do you mean? He isn't doing anything on the side."

"You haven't noticed anything strange about him? Places he goes and the times he goes to them? Any international trips? Any phone calls? Or meetings?"

"Please, Odelia, you have to stop what you're doing.

This is too far over your head. Your father was a special ops commander. If he couldn't escape it, neither will you or anyone else."

Her shaky voice and building tears nearly undid Odie. Losing a child had to be one of the worst tragedies to overcome. The pain was too much for Alice, that much was obvious. She was having difficulty losing her daughter, and couldn't bear to face her own husband being the killer. And whether he had hired someone to do his dirty work or not, he was still the killer.

No matter how hard it was for Alice, Odie had to make her understand. "Alice, Frasier was murdered a few days ago."

Alice inhaled a shocked breath and stared at Odie. "What?"

"I think he knew Luis was behind his brother's death."

"But…but…he never told me."

"He didn't have a chance."

More tears pooled and spilled over onto her cheeks. "I didn't know what else to do. Luis discovered us and… and…Frasier wanted me to move in with him. He said he'd divorce his wife if I divorced Luis. But I was afraid." Her gaze traveled around the richly appointed room. "I was afraid."

Engineers made good money but she was well-off with Luis.

She sobbed for a minute and then sniffled and looked up at Odie. "I loved him. I did. H-he gave me things that Luis never could. Affection, I mean. But I love Luis in a different way."

Sometimes people confused love with money. Money gave women security. If a man was providing it, then he might be the love of her life. Odie preferred to make her own way. Her money was hers right along with her successes. She didn't want to live through her man's successes. She defined herself; a man did not define her, and never would.

Odie stood and went to get a tissue from the end table. She returned with a few and handed them to Alice. "I'm so sorry, Alice."

Alice took the tissues and dabbed her eyes, quietly crying now.

"I should have gone with him," Alice said through her crying.

"You did what you had to do. None of this is your fault. Remember that."

That seemed to calm her tears. She looked up at her. "What will you do now?"

"I don't know," she lied.

Alice blew her nose.

"Will you be all right?" Odie didn't want to leave her but she didn't have much time.

After her blank gaze passed around the room, she looked up at Odie. "Y-yes…of course."

"Call me if you need anything. In the meantime, maybe you should find a place to stay for a while."

Alice nodded unsteadily. Odie reluctantly walked toward the door.

"Odelia."

With her hand on the front door handle, Odie turned her head to look back.

"I'm afraid."

Now that Odie could no longer deny the truth, she could see how weak Alice was. Women like her allowed men to rule them. Own them. Rob them of their independence. And men like Luis needed women like that. So they could get away with horrible things and still keep a wife. Luis was a man who wore two faces. One, the loving husband and long-time family friend, the other a self-gratifying devil.

"I'm not," Odie replied, and left.

Sitting in the backseat of the cab, she told the cab driver to take her back to the hotel. After that, he'd take her to Hersch's office, where she'd retrieve whatever data her key logger had busily gathered. Then she would take Luis down. She didn't care what it took.

Jag checked his watch. About a half hour had passed since Odie had left.

"We should go," he said to Calan.

They were still at the restaurant, and had just finished discussing the situation and going over viable action plans—the biggest one centered around Odie. Damn her. He had to agree with Calan that she was unpredictable right now. Odie emotional was new territory for anyone who knew her. That made her dangerous. It also made her a danger to herself. If she went to Raybourne by herself, what would he do?

He thought about calling Cullen but decided not to. Not yet. If she went off the deep end in a really bad way, then he would. He wouldn't put it past her to find a gun now. And he'd probably need backup.

"Where to?"

"Find Odie." Jag stood from the booth and started toward the exit.

Calan was a half step behind him. "You know where she went?"

"I have an idea."

"Getting to know her pretty well, huh?"

"I just know how she operates."

"Independently?"

Jag smiled but it was with much chagrin. "Very."

Calan chuckled. "You're a lucky man."

Lucky? "I don't think that's the word I'd use." Cursed, maybe, to be the man to fall in love with Odelia Frank.

"There aren't many women who match men in our line of work, but she seems to. Her background certainly suggests it."

Match him…

And what were those thoughts about love? He pushed them aside when he realized what Calan had said.

The man had lost two women the same way. Both murdered—probably by the same man. Jag couldn't imagine the anguish.

"I'm sorry about Kate," Jag said.

"She was an amazing woman. A lot like Odie in many ways. Not as brash, though."

Brash. Now there was a word to describe her. Jag chuckled. "And you think I'm lucky."

Calan didn't return the humor. "Better you than me. I'm done with women for a while. It just hasn't worked out for me."

Better off a loner. So many guys in this job leaned toward that, some not by choice.

"The right one will come along."

"I've already had two. What do I have to do? Have nine lives?" He shook his head. "No thanks. I'm on sabbatical. Maybe a permanent one."

Jag could see how his past would make him feel that way. If he'd lost two women he loved, it would jade him, too.

Entering the atrium, Jag saw the reporter who'd followed him and Odie amongst a cluster of plants and trees. He sat on a sofa reading a newspaper, or pretending to. Jag swore under his breath and stopped, holding his arm out so Calan did the same.

"What's the matter?" Calan asked.

"Reporter." He nodded toward the sofa where the reporter was looking over the top of the newspaper toward the elevators. He hadn't seen them go into the restaurant and was waiting for him and Odie to come down from their room.

"Why is there a reporter here?"

"Long story. Let's go out another way."

Jag led him down a hall near the checkout counter and followed the signs to the parking garage.

"Is he following Frasier's murder?" Calan asked.

"No, he's following Odie and me."

"Looking for a story?"

"One he hopes will lead to Cullen, I'm sure."

Calan nodded. "That's right. Odie was in the news back when he rescued that woman from Afghanistan."

"Now you see our problem."

"Now I see *your* problem."

Jag drove them to Alexandria and pulled to a stop in front of Senator Raybourne's house. A car drove past but there was no one on the street. It was beginning to get dark. He and Calan walked to the door. Jag knocked. When no one answered, he rang the bell. Still, no one answered. There didn't appear to be any lights on.

He glanced at Calan.

"You think she's already come and gone?"

"Maybe." He tried the knob. It wasn't locked. He looked at Calan again.

"Something doesn't feel right," Calan said.

And Jag agreed. His instinct was yelling a warning at

him. He reached under his shirt for his gun. Calan did the same, covering Jag as he entered first.

The house was dark and quiet.

Calan covered Jag as he went from the shadowy great room and kitchen area to a den and two guest rooms. Jag climbed the stairs to the second level ahead of Calan. On the landing, Jag covered Calan as he entered another bedroom.

Groaning coming from the room at the end of the hall made Jag hurry there. He entered the master bedroom. Lying on the floor, Alice was tied and coming out of a stupor. Tucking his gun back into his pants, Jag turned on a light and knelt beside her. He checked the bloody cut on her temple before untying her wrists.

She blinked up at him, obviously still disoriented.

Calan untied her ankles.

"Are you all right?" Jag asked.

Alice propped herself up onto her hand, sitting on her hip with her legs curled. She rubbed near the cut on her temple and eyed him.

"Who are you? You look familiar." Then she blinked some more. "You're that man Odelia was with. You came to my Kate's funeral."

"What happened here?" Jag asked.

Her breathing became more erratic, as if she only just then remembered why she was sitting on the floor of her bedroom with a cut on her head.

"Luis…he came home and he…" Her eyes widened. "He heard me talking to Odie. She told me Frasier was killed and…and…and Luis…we fought and then he…he hit me."

"Where is he now?" Calan asked.

"He—he's going after her. You have to hurry." She began to cry. "I'm so sorry."

"Where? Where did Odie go?"

"I…I don't know. I think Luis was going to go to the hotel where you're staying with her."

Jag doubted that. More than likely he'd get Hersch to send someone else after her. Just as he'd done before.

"I confronted him about everything Odelia told me," Alice said. "Sage's mission, Frasier's death. And Luis's involvement. He was furious by the time he left. He said he was coming back to take care of me when he finished with Odelia."

Why didn't he just kill her before he left? Maybe he loved his wife and hoped to browbeat her into submission. Dangerous. Alice could go to the police anytime. More likely he'd have Hersch take care of her. Unless he was beginning to realize he was reaching the end of his rope. How many more people did he think he could get away with killing?

"What did Odie say about Luis's involvement?" Calan asked. He stood to Jag's right.

"She said she didn't believe you were responsible for everything, Luis was. I should have listened to her. I didn't want to believe he was capable of…" She broke down into tears.

"She believed Luis was behind all this?" Hope soared in Jag.

Alice nodded through her tears. "I should have never broken up with Frasier. We could have gone somewhere for a while, just until this all went away. He'd still be alive now."

"You have no way of knowing that. Frasier wanted to avenge his brother's death as much as Odie wants to avenge her husband and father's, and now Kate's. You wouldn't have been able to stop him."

Alice sniffled and didn't look very convinced. "What am I going to do now? Where will I go?"

"I know someone I can call to watch over her while we're gone," Calan told Jag. "We can't leave her here alone in case Raybourne makes it back before we do."

But that wasn't what Alice had meant. She was alone without Luis. What would she do? "You're going to be all right," Jag told her. "Odie will make sure of it."

Calan made the call.

Where was Odie? He had to find her, Jag thought hard. Where would she have gone?

Her key logger...

She'd go get that first. Jag had left the visitor badge in the hotel room. He checked his watch. She'd probably already been there and left. So, she'd go to Hersch's and then the internet café. She wouldn't be worried about him catching up with her now. She was on their side. His side.

"Wait for me," Odie told the cab driver, handing him a hundred-dollar bill. "There's more if you do as I ask."

She'd told him to wait in front of the hotel, too, while she went in to get Jag's handy visitor badge. And now she'd asked him to park along the street in front of Defense Initiative.

He smiled. "Sure thing."

Leaving her laptop in the backseat, she got out and jogged toward the back of Defense Initiatives. It was getting late in the evening and this was ballsy of her to go in alone, without a gun. But she didn't really see a choice. Things were going to happen fast now and she didn't want to lose valuable information her key logger had recorded. If it had recorded anything. Hersch may not have done anything untoward on his computer in the last few days.

She took the same route to the shipping door. The badge worked like a charm and she silently thanked Jag for being so thorough. She was still mad at him for taking Calan's side earlier, but she didn't blame him. He'd seen the truth before she was able to accept it.

Upstairs, she heard the sound of someone tapping away on a keyboard. Someone was working late. She avoided that area and made her way to Hersch's office. Around the corner of a cubicle wall, she saw that his door was open and a light was on.

"Damn it," she whispered.

Ducking into a cubicle, she listened. He was talking on the phone but she couldn't decipher what he said. But then his voice grew louder. He was coming out of his office.

"I'll take care of it," she heard him say. "Meet me in the warehouse in one hour."

Who was he talking to? Had they alerted him to her presence? It didn't seem so. But she wouldn't take any chances. She had to hurry.

Odie leaned around the cubicle wall. Hersch held a cell phone to his ear and walked toward the front of the building. Rushing into his office, she stuck the key logging device into the USB port and waited a few seconds. The software would automatically download all it had recorded. She pulled the device out and went to the door. The hall was empty. Stepping out of the office, she headed for the stairs. In the shipping area, she glanced at the camera before pushing the door open. She broke into a run and sprinted all the way back to the waiting cab, looking around for anything out of place. It seemed clear.

"Downtime Internet Café," she told the cab driver, who checked the still-running meter and then eyed her in the rearview mirror. "Hurry."

He began driving. She glanced behind her through the rear window. There was a car, but she hadn't seen it when she'd gotten into the cab.

"Drive faster," she told the cab driver.

He eyed her in the rearview mirror again.

"There's more money if you do."

The cab sped up and she tensely waited out the ride.

When the cab stopped, she handed the driver a wad of cash. He smiled.

"Sure you don't need me to wait?" he asked.

"Yes, I'm sure." She didn't know how long she'd be so she'd let him go this time.

"Thanks, lady," he said when he saw her sizable tip, on top of the hundred she'd already given him.

Taking her laptop with her, she got out and looked up and down the street. Not seeing anything notable, she went into the internet café and paid for an hour. She found a seat that was relatively secluded and booted her laptop.

She put in the key logging device and scanned through Hersch's activity. He'd logged into his computer and email several times. The email was through a browser. Just moments before she'd gotten to his office to retrieve the data, he'd sent an email.

Getting too close. We need to move ahead of schedule.

Odie used Hersch's login information to get into his email remotely. Once she had the screen up, she sorted the emails to bring up all from the same sender.

There was an email thread arranging to meet.

We have a contract for Afghanistan. I'll meet you where we planned for the exchange. Do you have your end cleared?

It was vague and cryptic, but Odie would bet her thong underwear that it was Dharr. And Hersch's client had to be Luis.

Dharr replied with: Clear.

The next email read: There's been a delay. We have a problem with the Afghanistan contract. Someone is looking into L's affairs. Call me when it's safe and I'll explain.

The reply came back from the nondescript email address.

This deal is too important. Who is it? I will handle it.

Odie felt chills ripple over her arms and over her scalp. The someone looking into Luis's affairs was Kate.

Her name is Kate Johnson. Following that was Kate's home address.

We proceed as planned came Dharr's response. Dharr killed Kate. Luis hadn't given the order. But he'd told Hersch and that was the same as assuring her death.

Hersch responded with: Everything will be shipped to M-EX by the end of next week.

Odie checked the date. Just three days before Kate was killed. Hersch must be planning to ship tomorrow for a Friday delivery in Albania. From there the arms would be transferred to Afghanistan, where Dharr had somehow managed to make it appear as if the arms were going to a legitimate military force.

Odie forwarded all the emails to Cullen. Maybe he could trace their origin.

She searched through the other emails but found nothing of value. Shutting everything down, she put her laptop in its case and headed for the exit.

She paused at the door and scanned the street, wishing she'd have told the cab driver to wait again. She didn't see anything out of the ordinary. No familiar cars. No strange men lingering here or there.

Pushing the door open, she walked to the curb and looked for a cab. She saw one and waved. Just as it pulled over, she spotted a man standing across the street taking pictures. Of her. It was the reporter. Glad the cab had arrived, she got in.

"Grand Hyatt," she told the driver. He started driving.

Looking back, she saw the reporter hadn't moved, but still watched. She relaxed against the seat, but then noticed the driver was slowing to a stop.

"What are you…?"

Two men got into the backseat, one on each side of her. One of them pushed a gun against her ribs. The other was Hersch.

Chapter 11

Jag parked in a handicap spot and left the rental running as he got out and headed for the internet café. Calan was behind him. It was the same internet café he'd found Odie in before. He didn't see her through the front windows and got a bad feeling.

Inside, he went to the counter where a young man stood watching their approach.

"We're looking for a woman who may have been here. She's on the tall side, dark hair, blue eyes."

"Beautiful. Nice body," Calan added.

Jag sent him a warning look.

"Yeah, there was someone in here like that. She had a laptop with her. Just left a few minutes ago, caught a cab out front."

"Thanks." Jag left the café and stopped just outside, scanning the street.

He saw nothing unusual, but his gut told him something different.

"Isn't that the reporter?" Calan asked.

Jag followed his gaze to a car parked across the street. He headed there. The reporter started his car. Jag must've looked ominous or something because the guy seemed scared.

At the driver's door, Jag made a roll-down-your-window gesture with his hand.

The reporter eyed him dubiously and lowered the window three inches.

"Where did she go?" Jag demanded.

"What's it worth to you?"

"Your broken nose if you don't tell me."

The reporter contemplated him for a moment. "I want an exclusive on her. She does an interview with me."

"No deal. Where is she?" He was getting pissed.

Calan moved to the front of the vehicle. Now the reporter would have to drive over him to get away.

The man noticed and looked up at Jag. "I know you two are up to something and it's more than a family friend's murder. That's only part of it. What's going on? Are you investigating Defense Initiatives? What did Frasier Darby know about it?"

"I don't have time for this. You tell me where she is right now and nobody gets hurt." He lifted the hem of his shirt so the man could see his gun. "My friend has one just like it."

The reporter looked from the gun to his face.

"I'll break this window and shove it in your mouth in two seconds if you don't start talking," Jag said.

"She left in a cab about fifteen minutes ago," the reporter relented. "Two other guys got into the cab after she did.

They left their car parked over there." He pointed to a black sedan not far from the internet café. "It's the same car that followed her after she left Defense Initiatives to come here. It passed me when I was following her, too. I've been following her since she left the hotel."

"Did you call the police?"

"No, I wanted to find you. I was going to call the police if you didn't show up. But look, here you are."

Jag thought about breaking the window anyway to get his hands on the man. He didn't call the police because he was hoping to get a story out of this. Hersch and his men had taken Odie. Her life was in danger and this little puke had done nothing.

Where was she? Jag looked up the street, wishing he knew. Not knowing would cost him too much time.

He turned back to the reporter. "You better hope she's okay. If anything happens to her, I'm coming after you."

The man's eyes widened a little and he looked from Jag's clenched fists to his face again. "I know where they took her."

"Why didn't you say something?"

The reporter didn't answer. A story. He wanted a damn story.

Jag pulled his gun free and raised it, ready to bash the window.

"They took her to Defense Initiatives."

"How do you know that?"

"I was standing on the sidewalk when they paid the taxi cab driver to give them his car. One of them told the new driver of the cab to take her to DI. I'm assuming that means Defense Initiatives."

"They didn't see you?"

"I had my camera. I pretended to take pictures and not notice. They didn't bother me."

"Thanks." Jag started back toward the rental.

"Hey, wait!" The reporter got out of his car and stood on the sidewalk. "What about my interview?"

Jag kept going.

"What does Defense Initiatives have to do with Frasier Darby and Colonel Roth?" the reporter yelled.

Jag reached the rental.

"Do you want me to call the cops now?" the reporter yelled again.

Jag didn't care what he did. He had to get to Odie, fast. He got into the rental. Calan slammed the passenger door shut.

"He's awfully eager to splash you and Odie all over the news."

"It would be a boring story."

"I'm not so sure about that. You both work for Cullen McQueen, who's still in the covert ops business, breaking international laws and pissing off foreign diplomats who know it's the U.S. government in disguise when someone newsworthy ends up assassinated."

"You pay too much attention to the media." Jag drove fast down the street, blowing a stop light on the way.

"You going to marry her?"

Jag swung a glance over to Calan, startled.

"That's what I thought," Calan said.

Was it that obvious that he wanted her? Not to marry, it was physical with her. Now. What if he continued to see her after this was over and they went back to Roaring Creek?

Did he want that? He didn't see how it would work. He'd go on other assignments and be gone for months at a time.

She'd remember why she swore off special ops men and that would be the end of that.

Why put himself through the agony?

Because she might be worth fighting for...

He'd never met a woman who made him strive to work so hard to get her. She wasn't like his ex, not at all. She was someone he could be with permanently. But could he put his heart that far out for her? He trusted her on a professional level, but on a personal one? She might be honest and forthcoming, but would she let herself love him?

Did he love her?

He was afraid he was starting to. Odie was tough. Nothing brought her down. She was beautiful and smart. But he had to protect himself. He had to be sure she felt the same and wouldn't go running once she got in too deep.

"You're still thinking about it, aren't you?"

"You've had your fun. Let's focus on what needs to be done here."

"I am focused. Are you?"

Jag glanced over at him again. Calan was right. "I am now." No more thinking about a future with Odie. If he was going to save her he had to stop getting distracted.

Hersch's man gripped Odie's arm and dragged her out of the car. He was wiry and tall but very strong. He had white hair and looked to be in his early fifties. His light blue eyes were creepy and lined by deep, sagging wrinkles. He wasn't aging well and course white hair peeked out from the top button of his shirt. She thought about fighting him, but the driver was already out of the cab, aiming a pistol at her head. He was shorter than the hairy one, and more muscular. Younger, too, with dark brown hair that hadn't begun to gray yet.

"Bring her," Hersch ordered.

His man yanked her into a walk beside him. The driver followed. They were at Defense Initiatives, heading toward the loading dock and shipping entrance. Inside, they brought her through the shipping area and turned left where the building opened to a sea of cubicles. Forced to walk along the outer edge of the cubicles, they reached the far corner where double doors were secured by a keypad. Hersch entered a code and the lock released to allow them in.

Odie looked back over her shoulder as the doors closed and the lock clicked back into place. If anyone were able to find her, they'd have a hard time getting past that.

The man holding her jerked her. "Get moving."

She stumbled and faced forward. They were in a small warehouse. There were crates stacked in the middle and not all the florescent lights were on, so it was dim. There was a single rolling service door that opened to what must be the loading dock she and Jag had passed on their way in to the shipping area.

The man holding her shoved her. She tripped and regained her balance, but ran into a crate.

"Have a seat," the man said. She sat on the crate and looked from him to his two henchmen.

"We'll have a little conversation while we wait," Hersch spoke this time.

What was he waiting for?

"The first thing you're going to tell me is what you took from my office."

"Nothing." It didn't matter if he knew, other than the risk of him killing her in a fit of rage. She'd already sent everything to Cullen.

"I have you on recording entering and leaving my shipping room. You used a visitor badge. Now, I suggest you start talking."

"What are you waiting for? Or should I ask who?"

"What did you take from me?"

She didn't answer.

Hersch nodded at the man who'd hauled her here. He fisted his hand and swung. Ducking out of the way, she dodged his blow and sprang to her feet, kicking the side of his knee. He went down, his gun sliding across the concrete floor. It was too far away from her.

Odie pivoted, ready to fight.

The shorter man raised his pistol. Hersch stood calmly, his head angled mockingly.

The man she'd kicked climbed to his feet, anger making his eyes piercing. He favored his right leg as he went to get his gun. As he turned, he cocked the pistol and approached her, jabbing the side of her head with the gun when he reached her.

She met his furious gaze.

"Just say the word," he said to Hersch.

Hersch palmed the air, indicating for the man to lower his gun. "Not yet, Duke. Lower the gun. Give the girl some room for air so she can talk freely."

"I'm going to enjoy killing you." He lowered the gun and stepped back.

If only she'd picked up a gun before going to Hersch's office. She'd already be on her way back to the hotel.

Hersch moved closer to her. She faced him, ready to defend herself if necessary.

"I know who you are," he said.

Had Luis spoken with him? The senator didn't know what kinds of missions TES operated, but because of Kate he knew they were geared for counterterrorism and that they were all covert. He could do a lot of damage. Did he know she was on to him? Maybe Alice had told him…

"You may think with your fancy training that you can get away with crossing me, but you should reconsider. You aren't armed, a surprising, if not foolish, decision on your part. You're outnumbered, and no one knows where you are. The wise thing to do is to answer my questions."

"Why, so you let me go?"

His lips slithered into a contemptuous smile. "What have you discovered and who have you told?"

What would he do if she told him? Kill her and go after Cullen and Jag and anyone else associated with TES? Lots of luck with that, she wanted to tell him. He wasn't going to let her go. He'd try to close every loose end to protect his business. But his loose ends were multiplying.

"It's over," she said. "You can't win. Even if you kill me, there will be others."

Hersch stepped in front of her and put his hand on her neck, squeezing his fingers. "What did you find and who did you tell?"

She lifted her chin, not trying to get away from his grip, just letting him know without words that she wasn't saying anything. And she wasn't afraid.

"You went to an internet café. So you must have sent something to someone. Who was that?"

If Luis had told him who she worked for, he already knew. Or maybe he needed more specifics. Even Luis in a panic knew better than to reveal Cullen's identity. He didn't stand a chance against him.

"Someone you can't touch," she said. "And someone who will finish what I've started."

He stepped back. "Then there's no point in talking further."

He gave a nod to his two henchmen. The shorter one still aimed his gun at her. The taller one just smiled.

Jag got out of the rental with Calan and they walked toward the entrance of Defense Initiatives. Exterior lighting illuminated the landscaped grounds. Trees and shrubs curved in front of the building and a few cars were parked in the meagerly lit parking lot.

"Are we just going to walk right through the front door?" Calan asked.

"Yes. If she's here like that reporter said, Hersch would have taken her somewhere secluded." Like a basement or something. Somewhere that would be easy to clean up and hide evidence. He didn't like the thoughts that provoked... Odie being killed. She probably thought she could defend herself on sheer will alone, and if she got a hold of a gun she'd be an opponent to reckon with. But she wasn't skilled in operations. Her expertise was intelligence. She didn't know how dangerous people like Hersch could be, especially when their livelihood was threatened.

They had to find her. Fast.

"It won't be hard to disable the security guards and I doubt Hersch is expecting us this soon," Jag said, thinking aloud.

"Right." Calan pushed the door open and walked into the building.

A single security guard sat behind the reception desk. He looked up from his computer screen and saw them.

"We're closed."

"We know," Calan said.

"Do you have an appointment?"

Thanking the universe for their luck in having to deal

with only one guard, Jag didn't waste time and went around the counter, slipping his hand under his shirt for his gun.

"Hey," the guard said, standing up. "What are you—"

Jag raised his weapon and gave the man a hard chop on the back of the head. The man fell.

Dragging the man into the men's bathroom near the reception counter, he joined Calan where he waited by the door leading to rest of the building.

It was quiet on the upper level. Calan walked behind Jag but on the opposite side of the hall along a six-foot wall of cubicles. Ahead, Hersch's office door was open, as if he'd left in a hurry and forgot to turn off the lights and lock up.

Jag peered inside and swept the room with the aim of his gun. Giving Calan a nod, he resumed his careful steps toward the stairs.

At the bottom of the stairs, Jag checked the shipping area with Calan covering him. It was clear. There were no sounds of struggle. No voices. No screams. The lights were turned low.

The sound of rolling wheels penetrated the silence. Jag popped his head around the entrance to the shipping area. A janitor rolled a trash container around the corner of a cubicle wall, disappearing from sight. He hadn't seen Jag.

Jag nodded to Calan.

To the left, past a lengthy stretch of cubicle walls, were double doors secured by a coded locking mechanism.

"What's in there?" Calan asked.

Jag heard his sarcasm. He thought the same. That must be where Hersch had taken Odie. If she was here.

Please, make her be here and all right.

"It's probably a storage area or a warehouse, "he

whispered. "There's a service door next to the shipping door in the back of the building. Let's see if we can get in that way."

Calan followed him back through the shipping area, to the back doors. Opening one, he saw a rolling steel service door.

Headlights made him stop.

"We have company."

Jag recognized the car from Kate's funeral. "It's Senator Raybourne."

Letting the door shut, he and Calan waited, each on opposing sides of the double door shipping entry. Hearing the overhead door slide open, Jag opened the door in time to see the senator walk inside. It was dark except for a single outdoor light above the shipping door. But that light faded to shadows at the rolling door. Leading Calan, Jag held his gun up and put his back against the building at the warehouse entrance. A quick look revealed it was full of stacked crates.

Raybourne disappeared around a group of them. Jag and Calan slipped inside just as the rolling door began to close.

Odie saw where the tall man went to press a button to close the rolling door. There was her way out. If she could only get there.

Spotting Luis emerge from around a group of crates, she met his eyes. He saw her and quickly turned to Hersch.

"This has gone on long enough," he said.

"It's about time you got here," Hersch said, ignoring him.

"This is out of control," Luis persisted, coming to a stop beside him. "It stops here."

"It's too late for that. Dharr is expecting this shipment on Friday. I'm going to see that it gets there."

"You're a fool if you think you can pull this off now."

"You're only just now coming to that realization?" Odie asked.

He turned somber eyes on her. "You were always so tenacious. I had to keep a close eye on you. And I had a feeling it would only be a matter of time before you stuck your nose where it didn't belong."

"You mean after you murdered my father?" she spat. "Your *friend*?"

"I regretted that, too. You have no idea. It wasn't easy for me. Sage knew about Hersch's dealings with Dharr, but it was your father who discovered someone in the government was helping him. I couldn't let him piece it together. He would have, too."

"Yes, he would have." So much anger toiled around in her core she had to force her composure to remain stoic. "First Sage, then my father. And *Kate*." It was appalling. "How could you?"

"You don't understand."

"You're right. It's hard to understand how an old family friend could murder everyone close to him."

"I didn't murder anyone. A lot of this is out of my hands." He glanced at Hersch. "It always has been."

So Hersch had made most of those calls? He'd ordered the murders? She knew from the emails she'd read that he'd at least allowed Kate's.

"You went along with it."

"I have an equal stake in this."

"How many people do you think you can kill to keep your secret? Me? Everyone at TES?" she scoffed. "You can't kill everyone. Eventually you're going to get caught."

"What did you send to him?" Luis asked, and she didn't miss how he carefully left out Cullen's name.

"Everything. This is over, Luis. You're finished." She faced Hersch. "And so are you."

The tall man pressed his pistol against her temple.

"Wait." Hersch held his hand up. And to Odie he asked, "How did you find out about me?"

How could she answer that without revealing TES's inner workings. She couldn't. So instead, she looked at Luis.

"Calan Friese was there when Sage's mission failed," Odie said.

His eyes narrowed a fraction.

"He knew someone let the details of the mission leak to Dharr, who arranged the ambush. He thought it was my father, thanks to your clever setup, but then you tried to set him up the same way, only this time with Frasier Darby's forged letter."

"Calan?" He looked stunned.

"It's time to stop, Luis. You won't get away with taking bribes from Hersch anymore. I sent proof to someone you can't overpower. By now the right people at Army Special Operations Command know what you've done." She sent Hersch a smug look.

"Kill her," he said.

Odie stepped back from the tall man and his raised weapon.

"No!" Luis shouted. He sprang at the tall man, plowing into him and taking them both to the concrete floor. The gun went off. Odie stepped on the tall man's wrist and bent to pry the gun from his hand.

More gunfire made her flinch. She stayed crouched and saw the shorter henchman fall lifeless to the floor. She searched for the gunman and spotted Jag emerge from around the group of crates.

Her heart swelled with love. He'd had her covered the whole time.

Hersch backed up as Calan and Jag neared. He put his hands up. He wasn't armed.

Odie straightened as Luis rose to his feet. She aimed the pistol she held down at the tall man, who glowered up at her.

Luis went to the shorter henchman and bent to pick up the gun still in his lifeless hand.

Calan swung his gun toward him. Luis faced them and looked at Odie.

"I'm so sorry," he said.

Sorry hardly cut it.

"When I found out Sage was on to me, I thought I was finished then. I didn't want him to die. But Hersch…" He turned a resentful gaze to that man.

"I did what you didn't have the stomach to do. If I hadn't we'd have lost everything."

"We." Luis grunted a derisive laugh. "It was never about *we*. I begged you not to kill Kate."

"You were only too eager to stop Edward."

"Because I was afraid. I was afraid after Sage discovered what he did, and I was afraid when Edward did the same." He returned his gaze to Odie. "I never wanted anyone to die. Please understand that."

"You're the reason they're dead," Odie said. How could he ask her to understand? "You might as well have pulled the trigger yourself on all three of them. Frasier, too."

He lowered his head, a defeated man. "I'm sorry." Then slowly he looked at her again. "When this started I had no idea it would grow into what it's become. It's more than Hersch. There are others who'll kill me."

"You don't have to worry about that. You're going to prison. You'll be safe there." She didn't even try to keep the sarcasm from her tone. "And I know all about Dharr."

Luis looked surprised.

"Bitch," Hersch hissed.

She turned to him. "And you won't have time to warn him."

The sound of sirens grew louder.

Luis glanced that way and then once again met Odie's eyes. "I'm sorry." With that, he lifted the gun and put it to his head.

"Luis!"

But he pulled the trigger.

The sound of his body slumping to the floor would forever be imprinted on her mind.

Chapter 12

"Late last night police were called to the scene of an apparent suicide in a warehouse at Defense Initiatives, an arms broker with U.S. government contracts," the newswoman began at the top of the hour. Odie looked up from dumping her toiletries into her bag. "Luis Raybourne, a senator on the U.S Senate Arms Committee, was found shot in the head just after ten last night. Tom McNeery is reporting."

The screen went to a sunny morning in front of the loading dock at Defense Initiatives, where Tom McNeery stood a few yards from where yellow crime scene tape barred the warehouse entrance. He was the reporter who'd followed Odie, and he'd caught up to them after the police had let them go last night. She and Jag hadn't revealed anything that couldn't be in the press, but she was still nervous about what he'd say.

"Thanks, Nancy," Tom turned to look at the closed door

of the warehouse. "Beyond that door is what I'm told is where some of Defense Initiative's military orders for arms are packaged and shipped. The company recently obtained a multimillion-dollar contract with the U.S. government to provide arms to Afghanistan. As of this morning, that contract has been suspended…" He introduced Odie as an ex-army captain, and Jag as her partner. He explained Nigel Hersch's ties to Senator Raybourne and Odie's relationship to him.

A picture of Odie appeared on the upper right of the screen.

She tossed her hairbrush into the bag and folded her arms, giving all her attention to the television.

"Here we go," Jag said, and only then did she realize he'd emerged from the hotel room bathroom to stand beside her.

The reporter talked about her and Cullen and speculated on the reason she'd been looking into Darby's murder. He detailed the links to her father and Sage—all leading up to Raybourne's suicide.

A picture of Jag appeared next to Odie's. "While Ms. Frank is ex-army operations captain, her partner began his career as a Navy SEAL. Sources say he moved on to paramilitary work with the CIA up until about three months ago."

"What the hell?" Jag exclaimed.

Odie silently echoed the sentiment. This could get bad for TES, especially if the reporter followed them to Roaring Creek. They absolutely could not allow that.

The reporter went on to include Calan Friese's background as a major with the army up until a few years ago, after which he disappeared.

"We need to get out of here," Jag said.

"Although there's no obvious signs that Frank is still working intelligence with McQueen, her close ties to ex-Delta types—some who've turned up dead—makes you wonder." He paused. "Tom McNeery reporting from Washington, D.C."

"Thank you, Tom. It certainly does seem like something clandestine is going on there. But maybe we'll never know for sure." The anchorwoman turned toward another camera. "Up next, what's in store for people in the south Caribbean with the approach of Hurricane Al…"

Odie looked at Jag. "Good thing Cullen insisted on a private jet to take us home. We'll have to be careful we aren't followed to the airport, though."

"Yeah. Would have done that anyway."

Odie finished packing. She was afraid she'd have to take a vacation for a while. Cullen wouldn't want her anywhere near RC Mountaineering after this. She wasn't ready to leave her intel work behind, but a little time off wouldn't kill her.

"Maybe we should skip going home and just take a trip to the Caribbean or something," Jag said, mirroring her own thoughts.

The idea of staying with him crept up on her. She hadn't thought about how she'd handle them once they got home. But going to a place like the Caribbean with him was… intimate and came with a sense of permanence. How did she feel about that?

"Or not," Jag said.

Her hesitation must have cued him to her uncertainty. But he didn't seem offended.

She just needed time to sort out her feelings. It was a big step for her to get involved with another man after walking away from the last one on the altar. And Jag was an operative like Sage.

"We have to meet with Cullen first," she hedged.

"Yeah, I know." He picked up his bag and headed for the door. She picked up her own and followed.

In the hall, she caught his tense profile.

"Jag, where do you see this going?"

"Why don't you ask yourself that question?" he said.

They stopped at the elevator. Where did she see them going? A jumble of mixed emotions assaulted her. Anxiety. Dread. Lamentation. Nothing scared her more than falling in love. For so long she'd adhered to her principle of steering clear of men who reminded her of Sage, believing it was best for her. But now she'd spent time with Jag and the way he made her feel had her questioning that for the first time.

She didn't know how to tell him how she felt when she didn't fully understand it herself. He wanted to pursue what they'd started. Butterflies tumbled around her stomach. She broke into a cold sweat.

And yet…she didn't like imagining giving him up.

The elevator doors opened and she followed him inside. Another woman was standing there, thin and average height with straight light red hair and wearing a light green-and-pink-colored sundress.

Odie would rather be alone with Jag right now. She eyed the woman before saying in a low tone, "Sage…you don't understand."

Jag swung his eyes toward her, and she realized her blunder.

"I'm sorry, I didn't mean—"

"It's okay." He cut her off. Disbelief changed to resolve. He understood where her confusion stemmed from.

This was all new ground for her. She needed time to sort it out.

And she realized she had. It stunned her. "Oh my God. I didn't mean it. I'm sorry."

The redhead in the elevator pretended not to be listening, but Odie knew better. She waited until the doors opened and they entered the hotel atrium.

"Sage."

Jag sent her another incredulous look and just kept walking toward the exit.

Damn it, she'd done it again! "I'm so sorry. I'm just a little mixed up right now."

"You think?" He pushed the door open harder than necessary and they stepped outside into the humid air.

Absurdly, she felt like laughing. "I'm not confusing you with Sage."

He said nothing.

"I'm not. Jag, I haven't felt this way since him."

That got to him. He faced her in front of the hotel and searched her eyes. Finally the tension eased from his eyes and he nodded. "Take all the time you need."

Was that goodbye, or was it his way of saying he'd wait for her? An ache expanded in her core.

Jag flagged them a cab and Odie resigned herself to an awkward trip home. At least Calan would be on the plane, too. They were going to need the distraction.

Back at TES headquarters, Odie looked over at Jag as he leaned against the wall with one ankle crossed over the other. She had a hard time keeping up with the teleconference Cullen had just begun. Jag caught her gaze, indifferent, just like he'd been when they'd first met. He kept his distance, but he was cordial. It hurt her. Sadly, she didn't have a clue what to do about it. In her intel work she was never at a loss for an action plan or something smart to say, but what happened with Jag had a way of sucking all that out of her. All that was left were her feelings for him, and right now, a yawning confusion prevailed that she didn't know how to unravel.

"Odie?"

She looked over at Cullen, who sat two chairs away. He pointed to the secure phone with the jab of his finger. Calan sat across the conference-room table from her and she saw him look away when she caught him watching her.

Berating herself for not paying attention, she listened to Roth.

"If we could have talked to Raybourne, we might have a better lead on Dharr," he was saying.

"We know about the Albanian export company. I say we start there," Jag said.

"It's the only place to start," Cullen said. "Hersch isn't going to talk. He'll be indicted and go to trial, but what does the government really have on him? Attempted kidnapping and fraud? He might get slapped for a little time, but nothing that'll hold."

"It isn't Hersch we should be concentrating on," Calan argued. "It's Dharr. The export company might lead us to him, since we know Hersch was helping him get his hands on arms."

"I agree. We don't know where to find him," Cullen said. "He moves around too much."

"It would help if we knew what Edward uncovered," Jag said.

"And Sage," Cullen added.

"I'll search his computer and do some digging where I can," Odie said. "I never thought to check them for anything unusual. After he died, I looked for pictures and other things like sentimental emails. Maybe he kept something of use."

"Good," Cullen said. "But you'll do it somewhere else."

He was still angry with her for not following orders. But his declaration stirred apprehension.

"You know that reporter is going to end up here one of these days. I can't have him seeing you anywhere near this building. I can't even have him knowing you live in the same town."

She rented her house and paid all her utilities and other bills under a false name so there were no records that would tie her to him.

"The media lost interest the last time we went through this," she said. "I'll disappear for a while and come back after it's safe."

"We've decided to open a satellite office, Odie." This came from Colonel Roth.

Odie looked down at the phone, numb with the knowledge that Cullen didn't want her here anymore, even though it should come as no surprise.

"You'll spearhead the opening. You'll be a sort of intel hub for the rest of the organization. Our soldiers will come to you for information instead of the Roaring Creek headquarters. It's safer that way, really. Diverts the attention away from Cullen. You'll still get your orders from him and he'll run the organization and all its missions in every other aspect. We just think it's a good idea that we separate our intelligence unit from our operations unit."

Odie couldn't argue. "What about Jag and Calan? The reporter saw them, too."

"They're in operations. It's easier for them to stay

invisible. All they have to do is leave for their next mission. No one will be the wiser. And they don't have to come to TES to get their orders. They can go through our new satellite office."

"TES-O, and TES-I," Cullen said. "TES Operations, and TES Intel."

"And you want me to do the start-up for this… satellite office." Odie looked at Cullen, mourning their separation.

"You never liked it here anyway, Odie," he said, his tone friendly as it had been before she and Jag had gone to Roth behind his back. "And I was thinking of doing this regardless of the media storm. It's time. TES has grown enough to warrant another office."

"And it'll grow even more," Roth said. "Our people are very pleased with how you and Jag handled Hersch, especially the way you took out Raybourne. Not much leaked to the press. Had anything more gotten out about Raybourne, we would have been taken down. But everybody's safe and business can go on as usual."

The way he talked about Luis cued Odie that there was more to Roth's relationships to him than friendship. "You knew Raybourne pretty well, didn't you?" she asked.

"We were friends."

"More than that." She looked at Cullen as it all came together. "He was behind TES, too, wasn't he?"

Several seconds of silence stretched.

"You're as sharp as Cullen always says," Roth said. "Yes, he and I conceived of the idea of an organization like TES, but somewhere along the line he deviated to the wrong side."

"That's why Frasier was afraid to go back to you after he

learned what Calan knew. He found out the two of you were friends. Calan said he met Kate at one of your barbecues and Raybourne was there."

"Clever girl," Cullen said. "I'm sure going to miss you."

"Stop it or you're going to make me want to give you a hug."

She'd worked with him for such a long time. He'd saved her after Sage died and given her purpose in life again. She was going to miss him. A lot. The realization stopped her for a second.

"Oh, my God," she said, gaping at Cullen. "I think I actually care about you."

Cullen's brow lifted.

"You actually mean something to me," she added with the same flare.

He chuckled. "I sense the Odie I know and love returning."

"You're like a damn brother to me." She made a disgusted sound. "When did that happen?"

"Probably right after you started teasing me mercilessly about Sabine." His eyes twinkled with a smile. "Don't worry, we'll still see each other. Just not for a couple of years."

She laughed. She couldn't help it. "No wonder you've always been so irresistible."

Glancing at Jag, she wondered why he was so quiet. Just like when they first met…

"Just do a good job and don't make me have to close TES-I."

She turned back to Cullen. By doing something stupid like going to see Roth? "I won't. You know that."

His eyes softened, humor fading. "Yes. I do. Now that your father's murder is solved, you can put it all behind you."

She wasn't so sure about that. Sage had been murdered, too. She looked over at Jag again. And now there was Jag.

"We have one more matter to address," Roth said.

"Yes." Cullen looked across the table at Calan. "If it wasn't for you, we may have never caught on to Raybourne."

Calan shrugged. "It was only a matter of pooling our resources."

"Exactly," Cullen said. "I just have one question I need cleared up."

"What's that?" he seemed genuinely curious.

"Why did you quit Delta?"

"I got tired of doing what I was supposed to do and never seeing progress. I guess I felt too restricted."

"Delta isn't all that restricted."

"When it gets down to the Dharrs of the world, any restriction is too much. I want to be able to pull the trigger without having to ask please."

Cullen smiled. Odie knew that smile.

Rolling her eyes, she groaned in teasing annoyance. "Oh, please. Not another one."

Cullen only laughed. "Calan, you're a perfect fit for TES. How would you like to come and work for me?"

"That depends."

"On what?"

"What my next assignment will be."

"Going after Dharr, of course. Don't ask stupid questions around here. I've got a pilot ready to take you home to get packed. Then you're going to Albania."

"I haven't even agreed to take the job yet."

"Yes, you have."

And Calan smiled. "I'm going to like working for you."

"Just don't get killed. I fire anyone who gets killed."

"Duly noted."

Cullen looked up at Jag. "You take a vacation like we discussed. In six months, once the media dies down, let's talk."

Jag nodded.

Odie looked from him to Cullen. When had they talked?

"This meeting is over," Cullen said before she could ask. "And for the record, nobody says the name Roth or goes to see him ever again, got that?" He met each and every one of their eyes.

"Yes," Odie said, while Calan nodded and Jag turned to go.

Why had he and Cullen talked? Was it just vacation plans or was there more?

Outside, Odie caught up to Jag before he reached his rental. He was leaving.

"Jag."

He stopped and turned.

"Where are you going?"

"You heard the boss. Vacation."

She tried to read behind his green eyes, but he was too good at shutting off his emotions—or was he shutting her out?

Her uncertainty hurt him. Did that mean he had feelings for her? The urge to throw her arms around him and start kissing him burgeoned up in her. But it was such a huge step for her. She felt confident it was the right step, but…

She watched him take in her hesitation and draw his own conclusion.

"Take care of yourself, Odie." And with that he got into his rental and drove away.

Odie stared at the disappearing car until it vanished around a curve in the mountain road. Her heart began breaking apart. And tears burned her eyes. What the hell?

"Yep, it was like that for me, too."

Blinking ferociously, she glowered at Cullen.

"You don't want to believe it, but it's right there staring you in the face."

"Don't make fun of this."

"Oh, you mean like you made fun of me?"

She had, damn it.

"You'll deny it until something happens to make you open your eyes."

"Oh, okay, you're so smart, why don't you tell me what's going to happen?"

"You'll see." Sticking a toothpick between his teeth, he turned his cheerful face away and began walking across the street, where Sabine stood just outside her bookstore.

What the hell did he mean by that?

She watched him step onto the sidewalk and take Sabine into his arms. They kissed. What they had was so incredible. She could have that with Jag.

Odie stiffened. Never before had she been so consumed with just how much she did want that with Jag. When watching Cullen and Sabine became too painful, she looked down the road where Jag had gone. Had her second chance for love just driven away?

Chapter 13

Parked across the street, Odie stared at the narrow red brick building in a row of other shops. She checked the address again. This had to be it.

Weird.

She got out of the car she'd just rented and started walking across the street. It had taken her a week to pack and move. She'd found a suitable apartment to rent about fifteen minutes from this address, and she was going to sell her house in Roaring Creek. All the activity and logistics of moving had kept her occupied but hadn't taken her thoughts off Jag.

So many times she'd reached for her phone to call him, to see how he was doing, what he was doing. Was he still interested in seeing her? Was she interested in seeing him again? But something always stopped her from calling.

Jag had once told her she scared men off before they had a chance to get close. She came on strong as a defense mechanism. He was probably right. She had a strong personality, and she used it to push men away. He'd seen that about her and slipped past those defenses. But he'd blindsided her with the suddenness of it, how quickly the attraction had caught fire. It had taken her a while to see that he'd helped her overcome what remained of her grief. She no longer needed to avoid men who reminded her of Sage. None of them would anymore, least of all Jag.

Odie stopped on the sidewalk and looked up at the sign above the building. Dad's. Cute. But a bakery? Cullen had told her the building would need some work, but he hadn't mentioned anything about a bakery. What did he expect her to do with this? He wanted her to run a business here. It could be any kind of business. It didn't have to be successful, he'd told her—it just had to be good cover.

Opening the door, she entered a small dining area filled with four round white-topped tables on a dark wood floor. A glass display and counter took up most of the back, behind which a double swinging door led to what must be the kitchen.

She heard noises coming from there. Had Cullen already arranged for some contractors to do remodel work?

Making her way around the counter closest to a hall leading to the restrooms, she reached the kitchen doors and pushed one of them open. Inside, she stopped short.

Jag worked in holey jeans and a dirty white T-shirt—in the middle of inventorying pots and pans, as far as she could tell. They were all scattered over a worktable that had stainless steel cabinets below. He looked up as soon as she entered and froze just like her.

"What are you doing here?" she asked.

"I could ask you the same thing."

"Cullen sent me here." He digested that and she wondered if he'd rather she'd come here for him. She hoped. "To open the satellite office."

Now he seemed confused. "This is my building. I'm opening a bakery."

"What do you mean? Did Cullen send you here, too?" Did he want them to work together? Why hadn't he told her?

"When I told him I wanted to get out of special ops, he made me an offer. He gave me a sizable bonus and a six-month paid vacation. If the bakery doesn't take off by then, I have the option of going back to work for him."

She was flummoxed. That's what he and Cullen had discussed? "I don't get it. This is the address he gave me to start up the satellite office."

Jag stared at her.

She stared back. And then her brain started working again.

Of course. Cullen was doing to her what she'd done to him when he'd fallen in love with Sabine.

Jag seemed to realize what had happened, too. He grinned. Odie started laughing.

So did he.

She walked around the work counter and went to where he stood. Seeing him again was exhilarating. More than that. It felt like love. Waiting for a weight to drop in her stomach, or some terrible feeling of fear to overcome her, she found that only joy took up residence inside her. She wasn't uncertain anymore. And she wasn't afraid.

"I couldn't stop thinking about you," she said.

He just kept looking at her.

"I should never have let you go."

"And now here you are, compliments of Cullen."

All right, so he still had doubts. "I just needed a little push."

He angled his head. "What are you saying?"

He probably wasn't used to her beating around the bush. She slipped her arms over his shoulders. "That I want this."

He put his arms loosely around her waist. "What do you want?"

"You." She glanced around the bakery kitchen. "This place."

"You want to run ops out of my bakery?"

"Yes," she answered, marveling how wonderful that sounded. It was perfect…in so many ways. "Did you name it?"

"Yes."

Dad's, in honor of his dad. "I love it."

"I'm not a replacement for Sage," he said.

"Thank God," she breathed for emphasis, but she understood why he felt the need to bring it up.

He raised one eyebrow and his look remained skeptical.

"Sage was reckless and he didn't want to settle down," she said. "He was happiest in the field. He loved me, but he couldn't stay in one place. I'm over him. I have been for a long time. You made me realize that. I just didn't face it until now."

He was starting to look a little more satisfied.

"You were right," she said. "I pushed a lot of men away, but only because I thought I wasn't ready to fall in love again. But I am ready. I love you, Jag. I'm in love with you like I've never been in love with anyone else."

His satisfaction began to glow. "The front of the bakery needs redecorating."

She smiled. So he was going to make her work for it. "And you want me to do that?"

"It's your satellite office."

"It's your bakery. Why do you want me to redecorate it?"

"Why do you think I opened a bakery in D.C.?"

She recalled him saying he had family in Denver, and the significance of his choice in location engulfed her heart. He knew how much she loved this city.

"Jag…"

"I don't know what I would have done with this place if you hadn't come here."

"I do."

"Cullen was banking on putting TES-I here."

Did it bother him that it had taken Cullen's intervention to snap her out of her stupor? "He knew I would stay here." The same way she'd known about him and Sabine. "He knows I love you."

His gaze roamed with pleasure over her face. He liked hearing that. She was too cozy in his arms to move away. "So where's my office going to be?"

"There's one behind me."

She leaned around his big shoulder and saw a white metal door. "Nice. Is it bulletproof?"

"With you in there it doesn't need to be bulletproof."

Laughing, she rose on her toes and pressed her mouth to his. He tightened his hold and held her closer. She loved the titillating sparkle in his eyes. They shared a long gaze.

"Say it," she finally demanded.

"You're a pain in the ass."

She laughed again. "Just say it. Be my hero."

His deep chuckle vibrated against her chest. "I love you."

"Do you?"

"Like crazy. As crazy as buying this place was, with only the hope that you'd come around."

"Cullen will be very happy."

"Not nearly as happy as I am."

Odie sighed, immersed in the rightness of it all. He and she. This bakery. Washington, D.C. She'd never dreamed she'd find this kind of happiness again, but here it was. Here he was, the perfect man for her. The love of her life…a TES operative.

Who would have thought?

Not her. But she wasn't looking back. Not without Jag.

* * * * *

ROMANTIC
SUSPENSE

COMING NEXT MONTH

Available April 26, 2011

#1655 THE FINAL MISSION
Conard County: The Next Generation
Rachel Lee

#1656 SHERIFF'S RUNAWAY WITNESS
Scandals of Sierra Malone
Kathleen Creighton

#1657 SEDUCING THE ACCOMPLICE
All McQueen's Men
Jennifer Morey

#1658 FIVE-ALARM ENCOUNTER
Karen Anders

You can find more information on upcoming
Harlequin® titles, free excerpts and more at
www.HarlequinInsideRomance.com.

HRSCNM0411

REQUEST YOUR FREE BOOKS!
2 FREE NOVELS PLUS 2 FREE GIFTS!

 Harlequin®

ROMANTIC
SUSPENSE
Sparked by Danger, Fueled by Passion.

YES! Please send me 2 FREE Harlequin® Romantic Suspense novels and my 2 FREE gifts (gifts are worth about $10). After receiving them, if I don't wish to receive any more books, I can return the shipping statement marked "cancel." If I don't cancel, I will receive 4 brand-new novels every month and be billed just $4.24 per book in the U.S. or $4.99 per book in Canada. That's a saving of at least 15% off the cover price! It's quite a bargain! Shipping and handling is just 50¢ per book in the U.S. and 75¢ per book in Canada.* I understand that accepting the 2 free books and gifts places me under no obligation to buy anything. I can always return a shipment and cancel at any time. Even if I never buy another book, the two free books and gifts are mine to keep forever.

240/340 SDN FC95

Name _____ (PLEASE PRINT)

Address _____ Apt. #

City _____ State/Prov. _____ Zip/Postal Code

Signature (if under 18, a parent or guardian must sign)

Mail to the **Reader Service:**
IN U.S.A.: P.O. Box 1867, Buffalo, NY 14240-1867
IN CANADA: P.O. Box 609, Fort Erie, Ontario L2A 5X3

Not valid for current subscribers to Harlequin Romantic Suspense books.

Want to try two free books from another line?
Call 1-800-873-8635 or visit www.ReaderService.com.

* Terms and prices subject to change without notice. Prices do not include applicable taxes. Sales tax applicable in N.Y. Canadian residents will be charged applicable taxes. Offer not valid in Quebec. This offer is limited to one order per household. All orders subject to credit approval. Credit or debit balances in a customer's account(s) may be offset by any other outstanding balance owed by or to the customer. Please allow 4 to 6 weeks for delivery. Offer available while quantities last.

HRS11

*With an evil force hell-bent on destruction,
two enemies must unite to find a truth that turns
all-too-personal when passions collide.*

*Enjoy a sneak peek in Jenna Kernan's next installment
in her original* TRACKER *series, GHOST STALKER,
available in May, only from Harlequin Nocturne.*

"**W**ho are you?" he snarled.

Jessie lifted her chin. "Your better."

His smile was cold. "Such arrogance could only come from a Niyanoka."

She nodded. "Why are you here?"

"I don't know." He glanced about her room. "I asked the birds to take me to a healer."

"And they have done so. Is that *all* you asked?"

"No. To lead them away from my friends." His eyes fluttered and she saw them roll over white.

Jessie straightened, preparing to flee, but he roused himself and mastered the momentary weakness. His eyes snapped open, locking on her.

Her heart hammered as she inched back.

"Lead who away?" she whispered, suddenly afraid of the answer.

"The ghosts. Nagi sent them to attack me so I would bring them to her."

The wolf must be deranged because Nagi did not send ghosts to attack living creatures. He captured the evil ones after their death if they refused to walk the Way of Souls, forcing them to face judgment.

"Her? The healer you seek is also female?"

"Michaela. She's Niyanoka, like you. The last Seer of Souls and Nagi wants her dead."

Jessie fell back to her seat on the carpet as the possibility of this ricocheted in her brain. Could it be true?

"Why should I believe you?" But she knew why. His black aura, the part that said he had been touched by death. Only a ghost could do that. But it made no sense.

Why would Nagi hunt one of her people and why would a Skinwalker want to protect her? She had been trained from birth to hate the Skinwalkers, to consider them a threat.

His intent blue eyes pinned her. Jessie felt her mouth go dry as she considered the impossible. Could the trickster be speaking the truth? Great Mystery, what evil was this?

She stared in astonishment. There was only one way to find her answers. But she had never even met a Skinwalker before and so did not even know if they dreamed.

But if he dreamed, she would have her chance to learn the truth.

Look for GHOST STALKER by Jenna Kernan,
available May only from Harlequin Nocturne,
wherever books and ebooks are sold.

 **Harlequin**®

ROMANTIC
SUSPENSE

Sparked by Danger, Fueled by Passion

SAME GREAT STORIES
AND AUTHORS!

Starting April 2011,
Silhouette Romantic Suspense will
become Harlequin Romantic Suspense,
but rest assured that this series will
continue to be the ultimate destination
for sweeping romance and heart-racing
suspense with the same great authors
you've come to know and love!

Harlequin *Romance*

*Don't miss an irresistible new trilogy
from acclaimed author*

SUSAN MEIER

babies

IN THE BOARDROOM

Greek Tycoons become devoted dads!

Coming in April 2011
The Baby Project

Whitney Ross is terrified when she becomes guardian
to a tiny baby boy, but everything changes when
she meets dashing Darius Andreas, Greek tycoon
and now a brand-new daddy!

Second Chance Baby *(May 2011)*
Baby on the Ranch *(June 2011)*